Lead to the Head

Slocum dismounted and the butt of a rifle came crashing down on the back of his head, driving him to the ground.

"Told you he'd fall for the trick," said the man in the road. "It worked like a charm."

"Shut up. You for certain he's got the money?"

"I saw it back in Fort Smith. Ain't nowhere he coulda spent it 'tween there and here."

Slocum lifted his head and stared at the man in the road. He wore a mask, too, but there was no mistaking the shirt. He was the same man Slocum had encountered not a half hour earlier.

"He kin identify you," the outlaw with the rifle said.

Slocum turned in that man's direction just as the slug snapped his head back. Sight and sound faded away as Slocum lay sprawled on his back in the dirt.

JAKE LOGAN

SLOCUM
AND THE
BACKSHOOTERS

J

JOVE BOOKS, NEW YORK

THE BERKLEY PUBLISHING GROUP
Published by the Penguin Group
Penguin Group (USA) Inc.
375 Hudson Street, New York, New York 10014, USA

Penguin Group (Canada), 90 Eglinton Avenue East, Suite 700, Toronto, Ontario M4P 2Y3, Canada
(a division of Pearson Penguin Canada Inc.)
Penguin Books Ltd., 80 Strand, London WC2R 0RL, England
Penguin Group Ireland, 25 St. Stephen's Green, Dublin 2, Ireland (a division of Penguin Books Ltd.)
Penguin Group (Australia), 250 Camberwell Road, Camberwell, Victoria 3124, Australia
(a division of Pearson Australia Group Pty. Ltd.)
Penguin Books India Pvt. Ltd., 11 Community Centre, Panchsheel Park, New Delhi—110 017, India
Penguin Group (NZ), 67 Apollo Drive, Rosedale, North Shore 0632, New Zealand
(a division of Pearson New Zealand Ltd.)
Penguin Books (South Africa) (Pty.) Ltd., 24 Sturdee Avenue, Rosebank, Johannesburg 2196,
South Africa

Penguin Books Ltd., Registered Offices: 80 Strand, London WC2R 0RL, England

This is a work of fiction. Names, characters, places, and incidents either are the product of the author's imagination or are used fictitiously, and any resemblance to actual persons, living or dead, business establishments, events, or locales is entirely coincidental.

SLOCUM AND THE BACKSHOOTERS

A Jove Book / published by arrangement with the author

PRINTING HISTORY
Jove edition / January 2010

Copyright © 2010 by Penguin Group (USA) Inc.
Cover illustration by Sergio Giovine.

ISBN: 978-0-515-14741-4

JOVE®
Jove Books are published by The Berkley Publishing Group,
a division of Penguin Group (USA) Inc.
375 Hudson Street, New York, New York 10014.
JOVE® is a registered trademark of Penguin Group (USA) Inc.
The "J" design is a trademark of Penguin Group (USA) Inc.

PRINTED IN THE UNITED STATES OF AMERICA

10 9 8 7 6 5 4 3 2 1

1

John Slocum lay back, his head supported by his saddle, as he watched the fluffy white clouds moving slowly across the sky above Indian Territory. All that he needed for the day to be perfect was a small breeze to cool him down and keep the buzzing insects away. But mostly he thought the day was perfect.

He had a poke tucked into his shirt pocket close to five hundred dollars. He had worked hard for the money and then added a bit to it—added a lot to it—by judiciously choosing which poker games to join. He knew odds better than any of the farmers around Fort Smith. When his winning ways began to cause some grumbling, he left Arkansas, crossed the Canadian River, and kept riding west.

Indian Territory was slowly moving backward under his horse's hooves, and the summer weather was agreeable, if a touch on the sultry side. He had nowhere to be and no one to call a boss. His time was his, and he hadn't been this content in recent memory.

His horse nickered. He had tied the horse to a gum tree for both the shade and the lush grass growing underneath.

He sat up, wondering if the animal had tried eating some of the leaves and found a bitter taste that didn't suit it as well as oats.

Before he could go to see what bothered his mare, he heard what the long-eared horse already had. Somebody came galloping down the road he had just traveled.

"Mighty big hurry," he said softly, frowning. "Who'd want to kill a horse with that kind of hell-bent riding?" He slipped the leather thong off the hammer of his Colt Navy and turned a little so he could reach the six-gun in a hurry in its cross-draw holster, if the need arose.

Less than a minute later, a cloud of dust appeared back along the road, and then he saw the rider looking around frantically. When the man spotted Slocum, he drew back hard on his reins and brought the lathered horse to a halt only yards away.

"Top of the morning," the rider said.

Slocum nodded in the man's direction. His idea of a perfect day didn't include a traveling companion, but the rider didn't appear anxious to keep riding.

"You were in a mighty big hurry," Slocum said finally.

"What's that? No, nothing of the kind. T'ain't like me to hurry on such a nice day."

Slocum studied the man more closely and wondered why he was lying. The law might be on his tail. If so, it would behoove Slocum to take cover and let a posse ride past. He had a "Wanted" poster or two out on him—some were deserved, but the worst of the lot wasn't. After the war, he had returned home to Slocum's Stand, just wanting to recuperate from the wounds he had gotten at the hand of Bloody Bill Anderson, only to discover his parents and his brother, Robert, dead. Finding peace wasn't in the cards, though. A carpetbagger judge had taken a fancy to the farm and had trumped up fake tax liens. When he and his hired gunman had ridden out to seize Slocum's property, they had gotten more than they anticipated.

Slocum reckoned it hadn't taken long for the law to find where he had buried the bodies near the springhouse. A "Wanted" poster for judge killing had dogged his steps ever since. It hardly mattered to the authorities if the carpetbagger had been doing anything wrong. He had been a federal judge, and he and a deputy of the court had been murdered. That was all the law cared about.

There was scant chance anyone looking for the gent on the horse in the middle of the road would also be looking for him, but Slocum was a cautious fellow. He didn't want to ruin such a fine day by having to fight off the law or anyone else.

"Where are you headed?" Slocum asked. He shifted a bit more so he could go for his six-shooter if needed. The man on the horse noticed and wheeled his horse around so Slocum could see his right hip.

"I ain't armed, mister. No need to get all jumpy."

Slocum saw the sheen of the man's jeans where a six-shooter ought to hang. He might not be packing right now, but he had been not so long back. From the bounce of the saddlebags, he might have stripped off his gun belt and stashed his pistol there. Slocum wasn't sure why, but nothing about this gent felt right to him.

He was starting to get pissed at that, too, since it had ruined an otherwise perfect day.

"Where are you headed?" Slocum repeated.

"Just on up the road a ways. You want to ride along? We kin keep one another company."

"Not to be unsocial, but I'm not looking for a traveling companion," Slocum said. "I was just enjoying the fine day."

"Where you headed?" The question came out more pointed than the fake smile on the man's lips intended. "I mean, I kin rest a spell, too, if that's what it takes so we kin enjoy this fine day together."

"Ride on out and let me be," Slocum said. The man bristled at this. Slocum knew he wasn't a simple traveler along the same road because he didn't show any irritation in his next words.

"This part of Indian Territory is mighty peaceable, but the roads are long and winding. It's good to have someone to talk to as you while away the miles."

"Might be true," Slocum allowed. When he said nothing further, the man looked even more irritated but did not reply.

"Be seeing you," the rider finally said. He touched the edge of his dusty wide-brimmed black hat and rode on at a pace considerably slower than the one he had approached with. Slocum watched him go until he disappeared around a bend in the road. Lounging back, Slocum stared at the bright blue sky, but somehow it didn't give him the same feeling that it had earlier. The mood had been busted by the rider's intrusion.

Nothing about the man set right. Slocum was sure he had a six-gun hidden away in his saddlebags. Why not be open about wearing a piece? It wasn't any crime, not in Indian Territory or much of anywhere else outside the bigger cities. Slocum had heard Kansas City law was getting uppity about wearing a six-shooter, but that's what happened when a town got too big for its britches.

It was time to move on when things like that became law. And Slocum knew it was time to move on because lazing about seemed less likely to be a safe thing now. If the rider was on his way to reach others, it was likely they weren't up to any good.

Slocum saddled his horse and mounted. He walked slowly after the other rider, keeping an eye on both the tracks in the soft dirt and the road ahead. He reached a fork in the road and dismounted, dropping to his knees to study the tracks more closely. The rider had definitely taken the fork going due west. Slocum mounted and went to the northwest. If he remembered the country aright, this eventually led to Fort Gibson.

After ten minutes he relaxed and began to enjoy the day again, even the buzzing, biting insects swarming all around his ears. This lulled him into a complacency that he usually avoided.

"Stand and deliver," came the cold command.

Slocum jerked around, looking over his shoulder. A man with a bandanna pulled up over his face held a rifle on him. He heard movement on the other side of the road. A second road agent came into view, similarly masked but holding a six-shooter. Stepping into the road to block any possible escape Slocum might try was the rider who had taken the other fork—or so Slocum had thought.

He said nothing as he raised his hands.

"Git on off that horse."

Slocum lifted his leg up and over and dropped to the ground. The butt of the rifle came crashing down on the back of his head, driving him facedown onto the ground.

"Told you he'd fall for the trick," said the man in the road. "It worked like a charm."

"Shut up. You for certain sure he's got money?"

"I saw it back in Fort Smith. Ain't nowhere he coulda spent it 'tween there and here."

Slocum lifted his head and stared at the man in the road. He wore a mask, too, but there was no mistaking the shirt or that he wasn't wearing a holster. He was the same man Slocum had encountered not a half hour earlier.

"He kin identify you," the outlaw with the rifle said.

Slocum turned in that man's direction just as the slug snapped his head back. Sight and sound faded away as he lay sprawled on his back in the dirt.

A million ants gnawed at his flesh and brain. John Slocum groaned and tried to brush them away, but his hands refused to obey. He rocked to one side and thought his head was going to bust open like a pumpkin caught in an early freeze. He slumped back and lay faceup. The sun warmed the right side of his face. That didn't seem right to him. It should have been directly overhead.

"Don't take anything," Slocum mumbled. Even in his condition he knew it was hardly more than a whisper. His lips were chapped and his face ached. His eyes flickered open and stared into the setting sun. Reaching up, he touched the spot where the bullet had grazed his head. His fingers came away sticky with oozing blood. He sagged back, working his way through the pain in his head and the way his body refused to obey even the simplest of commands.

Forcing himself to roll onto his belly, he got to his hands and knees. Dizziness hit him and then passed enough for him to straighten and look around. He was alone. He was also without a horse, five hundred dollars in greenbacks, and his Colt.

Slocum got to his feet and wobbled. His vision was blurred, and his head was going to explode. He staggered off the road where he had been shot and found a shallow puddle of scum-covered water. He thrust his head into it and let the water refresh him. He wiped away the slime and then used his soaked bandanna to mop away the blood on the side of his head. Every touch was a nail driven into his flesh—and added to his determination to get even with the bushwhackers who had shot him.

The loss of the money irritated him. Taking his horse and his six-shooter infuriated him. Anyone who would gun down a man was a low-down, no-account snake. But taking his horse? Bad. As he started walking, one foot and then the other tromping down heavily, his strength returned. After he had walked a mile he had his plan mapped out in his head.

He'd take the road agents one by one. Without a pistol, he had to do it that way. He bent and ran his fingers over the horn handle of the knife thrust into the top of his right boot. They hadn't even searched him after they had stolen his money. That would be their second biggest mistake.

Their biggest mistake was crossing John Slocum in the first place.

Now and then as he walked he saw the hoofprints of their horses in the soft earth alongside the road. They rode abreast, and the road wasn't wide enough for them all to stay on the hard-packed dirt. He lost the trail when the sun finally set and the moonless night refused to give him a break.

He kept walking along the road. There wasn't any other way he could think of to find the sons of bitches who had shot him down and robbed him.

Less than an hour later his nostrils flared at the whiff of a campfire. The wood was a bit green and caused smoke to rise from the fire a few yards off the road, hidden by a wall of thick undergrowth. He turned toward the scent, got his bearings by the thick plumes of smoke rising to blot out the stars, and then carefully moved through the thorn bushes.

They tore at his skin, but he hardly noticed. He heard voices ahead. Voices he recognized.

"I swear, he was like a fish outta water. Didn't ya love the way he flopped around 'fore he died?" Hearty laughter echoed through the wooded area.

Slocum moved closer until he saw the campfire where two men huddled close, working to fix dinner and boil some coffee in a large pot. He stood stock-still as he tried to find the third outlaw. If he was out in the woods taking a leak or maybe hunting for something more to add to the stew pot, Slocum didn't want to get caught between him and the two in the camp.

"He did kick a mite, didn't he?" The second outlaw chuckled, then spat into the fire. The sudden flare caused Slocum to recoil. He thought the man might have spotted him, but instead the road agent pulled out a whiskey bottle and took a pull.

"Gimme some of that. We oughta celebrate."

Slocum sucked in his breath and held it. They were

celebrating his death. There wouldn't be any celebrating their deaths—Slocum wasn't going to laugh or boast after he killed them. He was simply going to slit their throats. He reached down and drew his knife.

"Where'd Kent git off to?" The first outlaw looked around, trying to pierce the shadows. Slocum froze as the man looked directly at him.

"Who cares?"

"Ain't like him to run off like this."

"Look, Harsch, you got the son of a bitch's gun. Kent took the horse. We split up the money. What do you care where Kent got off to?"

Harsch held up Slocum's Colt Navy and admired it.

The distance between the edge of the woods and the campfire was more than five yards, but Slocum had to do something after seeing the outlaw holding his very own six-shooter. He pushed through the undergrowth and started walking at a steady pace, neither hurrying nor taking his sweet time.

"That you, Kent? 'Bout time you—"

The road agent died when Slocum got close enough to drive the knife hard into his belly and lift the blade upward. A second thrust pushed the point into the man's heart. He died with a jerk and then sagged.

"Surely does flop around like a fish out of water, doesn't he?" Slocum asked as he turned.

Harsch was the one who looked like a fish out of water. His mouth opened and closed. He tried to lift the stolen six-shooter and fumbled. Slocum stepped over the fire and felt sparks along the side of his leg. He ignored the small hot spots and swung his knife in a broad arc.

He missed Harsch only because the man jerked away in fright. Slocum kept moving forward like an elemental force of nature, kicking Harsch's ill-gotten gains out of the way. He could reclaim his gear later—after he dispatched the road agent.

"You got it wrong, mister."

Harsch tried to swing Slocum's Colt around. The distance between them was too great for Slocum to reach the man, who still scuttled away. Slocum flipped the knife around and took the chance at throwing it. If he missed, he was weaponless and looking down the bore of his own pistol.

He didn't miss. The thick blade sank into Harsch's gut and produced a gout of blood that shocked the outlaw more than the pain. Slocum didn't give him a chance to think about what to do next since he still held the stolen pistol.

Slocum vaulted over his saddle and grabbed the deerhorn knife handle and twisted hard. This time Harsch felt the pain and knew he was going to die. A curse came to his lips and then died amid the blood bubbling forth. Slocum's toss had punctured a lung.

"You—" Harsch convulsively jerked and discharged a round. The report from the six-gun sounded like a cannon in the still night. Slocum grabbed Harsch's wrist and twisted hard. Bones broke, but Harsch did not care. He was already dead.

Slocum pried the Colt Navy from the dead man's grip and stepped back. He had his six-shooter in his left hand and the bloody knife in his right.

"What's going on?"

Slocum looked up to a dark patch of woods.

"Uh," he grated out, "Harsch drank too much."

He wiped off the knife blade on Harsch's shirt, tucked the weapon away, and then gripped his familiar six-gun, waiting. He wasn't sure his disguised voice was enough to dupe the third man.

"Move on closer to the fire so I can see you," Kent called.

Slocum judged where the voice came from and began firing. Three quick shots, one left, one right, one directly at where he thought Kent hid.

For a brief instant, Slocum believed he had removed the last of the outlaws. But then Kent stepped forward from the shadows and stared hard at Slocum, complete disbelief etched on his face.

Slocum lifted his six-gun and squeezed the trigger. The hammer fell on an empty chamber.

As if that were the cue to begin a footrace, Kent spun and plunged into the forest while Slocum cursed. He always rode with the hammer resting on an empty chamber, but there should have been a single round left. Harsch must have fired a second round, one that Slocum hadn't heard.

Slocum dropped to one knee and fumbled to pull the hogleg from the holster of the first road agent he had killed, intending to go after Kent immediately.

The pounding of hooves told him Kent was hightailing it. On *his* horse. That thought made Slocum madder by the minute as he took the time to reload his six-gun, then strip the dead outlaws of not only what they had stolen from him but a few dollars more.

Only then did he heft his saddle and go to find where Harsch and his partner had corralled their horses for the night. He had an outlaw to run down—and bring to leaden justice.

2

Slocum considered simply leaving the bodies for the buzzards and ants, but was hesitant to do so. He owed them nothing. They hadn't bothered considering a grave for him when they'd dry-gulched him. And if they had tried to bury him, he would be dead now.

Heaving a sigh, Slocum got to work digging shallow graves for the men he had killed. Insects had already worked their way into the men's bodies and flies buzzed about. He idly swatted them away as he worked. As he rolled Harsch into the grave with his partner, Slocum saw a scrap of paper sticking from the man's vest pocket. He had searched both and had missed this, hunting only for greenbacks and possibly specie.

He plucked the paper from Harsch's pocket and held it up. The light from the dying fire illuminated the writing enough for Slocum to make out the scribbles. He tucked the sheet away after reading it twice. If he wanted to get his revenge on the third outlaw, he'd have to ride fast and hard to overtake him. According to the instructions that had been written on the paper, these three were to meet with a larger gang in a day or two.

In a way, finding the note helped Slocum. He knew where Kent would head and would not have to track him in the dark. The downside of the outlaw joining the larger gang was that Slocum would have to cut Kent out from the herd to kill him. That might be a lot harder than it had been killing Harsch and his partner using nothing more than a knife.

He kicked the last of the dirt back over the two bodies, then stacked a few rocks on the dirt mound. It wouldn't keep a dedicated, hungry coyote from digging up the bodies, but it would have to do. Slocum wasn't in any mood to do a better job with the grave.

The coffee boiled merrily in its pot and the smell of the outlaws' vittles made his mouth water and his belly rumble. It had been a spell since he had eaten anything. He pulled out the paper again and reread the instructions. It wasn't a map, but it was mighty clear where the gang assembled. He could spare an extra fifteen or twenty minutes and get himself some grub, especially since the two road agents had already fixed it.

He spat most of it out in the fire. They couldn't even boil oatmeal so that it tasted good, but the coffee went down respectably, warmed his belly, and then spread some energy throughout his body for the ordeal facing him. He drank the dregs, started to gather the pots and pans, then stopped. There was no reason to take any of this. He had his own gear.

Slocum searched through his saddlebags and made certain Harsch hadn't bartered away any of his possessions. Hefting his saddle, he went to the crude corral the outlaws had built for their horses, saddled a stallion that looked strong enough to run, then used the end of his reins on the other two horses' rumps to get them running. There was no reason to take them along, though he could sell the pair for good money once he reached a town. Since this was Indian Territory and folks didn't ask too many embarrassing questions—such as where a single rider came upon two other riderless horses—he might have gotten a fair price. But it was better to ride as fast and as free as he could.

Getting his bearings from the stars, he headed toward the outlaw rendezvous at a good clip. He listened for other horses and sniffed the air occasionally to make sure he wasn't riding past the outlaw camp. All the directions had specified was northwest. Slocum assumed Harsch knew where the gang was gathered and had needed only the reminder.

He frowned as he thought on that. Giving only a direction meant whoever had written the note knew where Harsch and his partners were riding. Slocum wondered if he had stumbled onto something more organized than the usual outlaw band roaming the Indian Territory. It might be that the leader had sent smaller groups out to rob and pillage and knew how to instruct them to return when they finished. The trio Slocum had come across might have worked their way along the road, or simply had been stationed along the road to waylay and rob anyone unlucky enough to ride past.

He varied the horse's gait to keep from tiring it unduly. He thought the horse was in good shape but had been mistreated and it balked now and then whenever Slocum asked for a quicker pace. The stallion wasn't one he would have picked from a remuda had he been buying, but as a substitute until he got back his mare, it would do just fine.

Refusing to rest paid off for him. He heard the protests of his mare from a hollow not a dozen yards off the road. He knew the outlaw had ridden the mare until she refused to go on. Slocum had many more miles left in the stallion, should Kent try to run. Since he was so tired, Slocum vowed not to give the outlaw the chance.

He threaded his way through the sparse trees until he

came to the edge of a large clearing. Kent paced anxiously, looking all around as if he expected Slocum to come swooping down on him. Slocum pulled his Winchester from the saddle scabbard and levered a round into the firing chamber. The telltale sound alerted Kent.

He swung around, hand going for his six-gun.

"That you, Turner? That you?" Kent stepped away from the horse, giving Slocum a decent shot, in spite of the darkness.

His finger came back, then relaxed when he heard movement in the woods from behind him. At least a dozen riders came from the road, following a path parallel to the one Slocum had taken to reach this point.

A dozen thoughts blazed through his brain. Kent had reached the rendezvous, and the Turner Gang, if that was the right name for the leader and not just someone Kent knew or feared, rode to join him. The smart thing would be to simply fade into the darkness, let Kent keep the mare, and consider the score even with Harsch and the other road agent in their grave.

Slocum's finger came back fully on the rifle trigger. The stock bucked hard into his shoulder and he saw Kent crumple as if every bone in his body had turned to aspic.

"What's going on?" came the cry from Slocum's right. Whoever shouted the question wasn't ten yards off. Answers and more questions came from the rest of the gang.

In the middle of the confusion, Slocum urged his stallion forward and past Kent's fallen body. He wished he had time to recover the outlaw's third of the money stolen from him earlier, but already horses began appearing from the woods as if by magic. Slocum reached down and caught the dangling reins of his mare and turned its face. He rode away at a sedate pace, not hurrying and hoping that the dark would hide him.

He got to the far side of the clearing without any trouble. He dismounted, switched saddles, and mounted his mare.

She whinnied in greeting—and this was Slocum's undoing. The stallion, now free of a rider, reared and lashed out with its front hooves. The mare shied. Before Slocum could regain control, the stallion raced back across the clearing in the direction of the dim shapes now standing in a circle around Kent's body. Slocum cursed as two of the men helped Kent to his feet. He had winged the outlaw but hadn't killed him dead enough to stay dead.

"He went that way!" Kent pointed in Slocum's direction. The cry spread among the half score of men. They stepped up into their saddles, giving Slocum a moment to consider what he ought to do. He was still hidden in darkness, though they knew the direction to ride.

Seeing nothing to lose, Slocum began firing into the dark mass of riders galloping toward him. He didn't hit much, but from the sounds of pain and grunts of anger, he scared the horses and winged a man or two. He also revealed his position exactly. The foot-long tongues of orange fire leaping from the muzzle of his rifle might as well have been a signpost pointing directly at him.

When his magazine came up empty, he wheeled around and let the mare pick her way through the more heavily forested area he found himself in.

"He's ahead, boss. I see him!"

Slocum ducked but the bullets singing through the night went wide by several yards. The outlaws were veering away from him. He used his knees to guide the mare away at an angle. To simply stop and let them pass was something he considered for only a split second until he heard a rider directly behind him. The outlaw leader had sent his men out searching in a fan-shaped pattern, and the one at the farthest end was coming up fast on him.

"I got him. Here he is!" Slocum shouted. He slid his ebony-handled six-shooter from its holster as he waited tensely for the road agent to take the bait and gallop forward to his death.

The man proved warier than Slocum had hoped.

"Who's that? Who are you?"

"You fool," Slocum hissed, his hand turning sweaty on the handle of his gun. "Over here. I have him. He's on foot but he's getting away!"

In most gangs, there were always newcomers who rode for a job or two and then vanished. The cadre who stayed with the leader knew one another but were seldom familiar with any of those who drifted in and out with some regularity. Mostly, they didn't want to know because it was safer if they never thought of the newcomer as someone willing to watch exposed backs and be counted on in a fight. To Slocum's dismay, this man had to be one of the hard core of Turner's gang.

"Got 'em over here, boss. He's tryin' to gull me into a trap!"

Slocum fired several times. He heard wood splinter off tree trunks and leaves rustle as the lead passed through them, but nothing told him he had come close to even winging the outlaw on his trail.

The sounds from the rest of the gang worried him into action. He swung about and let his horse make its way through the woods faster than was safe. But staying where he was and trying to shoot it out was suicidal. Before he realized it, he burst from the wooded area and saw a road wandering away over a hill. Slocum put his head down and put his spurs to the mare's flanks. They shot off like a rocket and topped the rise in time for Slocum to look back and see a half dozen men emerge from the woods, shadows within shadows. One sharp-eyed outlaw spotted him silhouetted against the starry sky, and the chase was on.

Slocum couldn't hope to outrun the entire gang. He tried to count the men after him and gave up. They shifted positions as they rode and a dust cloud obscured them from time to time. He knew Turner rode with at least four men, maybe more. As he bent low, he tried to sort out the road agents he had killed and who might remain. Kent had not been among them. That meant one of Turner's gang could pick Slocum out.

He veered suddenly, let the mare jump a ditch filled with barely enough water to breed mosquitoes, and made his way toward a draw. He reined in hard and brought the horse to a halt. Slocum leaned forward to place his hand on the horse's nose to restrain an aggrieved whinny.

Hooves pounded in the road behind him. He had no way to count the men or to know if all of the road agents remained with their leader. One or two might have hung back. If Slocum had been giving the orders, that's what he would have done so his quarry couldn't double back without getting caught.

"There, there," he soothed. The mare finally allowed him to dismount without creating a ruckus. He let the horse drink from a muddy pool, then crop at the grass growing around it. The night was filled with the usual sounds. Insects buzzing, a hooty owl off in the distance, the wind listlessly stirring through the trees.

Slocum returned to the road and saw that he had quite a hike if he wanted to reach the ridge to the west where the road agents had ridden. He turned and let out an involuntary gasp when he found himself facing a drawn sixshooter.

"The boss thought you was slippery as an eel, so he told me to hang back and see if you were sneaking back on our trail."

"Is this any way to treat someone riding with you?" Slocum asked.

"What?"

"Kent'll vouch for me. Him and Harsch," Slocum said, turning slightly to present a smaller target. The outlaw was hesitant now. There would be a chance for Slocum to draw and fire if the man's gun wavered off target, even a hair.

"Harsch is dead."

"What happened?" Slocum jerked around, his left hand flying away from his body. The outlaw followed the movement with his eyes—and his six-shooter.

This was all the opening Slocum needed. He drew and fired twice before the road agent could swing his iron back onto target. The owlhoot dropped to the ground and kicked once before he died. Slocum cursed when he heard Turner and the men riding with him returning. They had either given up on the hunt or hadn't gone too far and were coming to investigate the gunfire.

Slocum raced back to his mare and vaulted into the saddle. The horse sagged a little under the sudden weight, then gamely headed straight into the dark woods. Slocum heard Turner screaming at his men but there was little chance they could find the trail in the dark.

By sunrise Slocum knew he had lost the Turner Gang and rode on, feeling better than he had in a couple days.

3

Bitter Creek looked mighty sweet to Slocum after spending the night dodging Turner and his gang. The sun poked up over the rooftops, promising another scorching-hot day. Unlike the day before when Slocum had taken time to laze about, he felt the need to keep riding and get the hell as far away from Indian Territory as he could. He never thought getting robbed would cause such a tornado of destruction all around him.

Slocum touched his pocket to reassure himself he had recovered most of the money. He had his gear, his horse, and his six-shooter, too. The few greenbacks he had lost were insignificant compared to the need to keep on living. As much as he wanted to recover what he had lost, he still had more than three hundred in scrip to spend.

His belly growled as he passed by a restaurant. The aromas gusting through the open door enticed him. He ate a hearty breakfast, then came out and looked around Bitter Creek. He had plenty of supplies, so there was no reason to linger here. As he stepped into the street and prepared to mount, he heard footsteps behind him. He froze.

"You here for the job?"

Slocum got his foot out of the stirrup and turned to face a portly man staring at him through half glasses that made him look older than he was. Although his dark hair receded and left a widow's peak, the round face made him out to be in his late twenties. From the cut of his clothing, he was prosperous.

"What job might that be?"

"Good," the man said. "Keep on riding."

"What job?" Slocum asked again, louder. This caused the man to rear up. He puffed out his chest as if this would intimidate Slocum.

"If you don't know, it doesn't concern you. Good day, sir!"

The man turned and bustled off, chin high, as if begging Slocum to take a poke at him. Slocum watched as the man went down the street and entered the bank. Everything about him screamed *banker*, making Slocum even more curious as to the job the man had mentioned. Given the aggressive pose, Slocum figured the job wasn't with this bank, and he didn't see another advertised openly. He had been caught in the cross fire a time or two when rival businesses got to feuding. Bitter Creek was hardly large enough for one bank, much less two. There had to be something more, but as curious as he was, he wasn't about to ask around. He wanted to get on the road and put a lot more miles between himself and the Turner Gang.

He rode slowly out of Bitter Creek, got on the trail, and kept his mare walking steadily for better than an hour. About the time he was ready to partake of water from a small stream running alongside the road, he saw a woman in the road ahead. She knelt beside a buggy canted at a crazy angle. As he watched, she half stood and grunted, trying to right the buggy.

Slocum ignored his mare's desire for water and walked up to where the woman struggled.

"Can I help, ma'am?"

She looked up and he got a good look at her face for the first time. His heart almost skipped a beat when he saw her beauty. Her oval face was streaked with sweat and dirt, but her bright blue eyes showed no hint of fatigue—or lack of determination. Her jaw was set firmly and her dark hair had been pulled back, fastened, and thrown over her left shoulder. In spite of the dirt, the lustrous midnight-black hair hung almost to her waist. Her clothing was the worse for wear, showing thin spots and occasional patches. At one time it had been a fancy dress, but it had been worn way too much.

Slocum guessed her luck hadn't just changed for the worse upon getting her buggy wheel mired down the way it was. The string of bad luck stretched back months and months.

"Would you be a Good Samaritan, sir? I have mired down and cannot get free."

Her speech was cultured, showing more education than most folks in the area.

"You from back East?"

"Only if you call St. Louis back East," she said as Slocum walked around the buggy to study the problem.

"Can you get in the buggy and whip the horse when I tell you?"

"Won't that cause the buggy to sink deeper?"

"I'm counting on it sinking down far enough to find harder dirt. You're spinning around and around in the mud." Slocum scooped some of the mud away and stuffed dried limbs collected near the road under the front of the wheels. When he finished, he got behind, put his shoulder to the frame, and told her to drive.

The buggy rocked once, twice, then the combination of Slocum's shoulder, the traction, and the horse pulling caused the buggy to pop free of its rut. The suddenness caused Slocum to drop to his knees and catch a spray of mud from the spinning buggy wheels.

"Oh, sir, I'm sorry. I never meant . . ."

Slocum wiped the mud from his face and shirt and had to laugh.

"I've gotten dirtier for reasons nowhere near as good. This isn't anything a quick bath won't cure."

"Sir, follow me to my farm. I'll gladly wash your clothes while you bathe. This is all my fault."

"Wasn't anybody's fault that it rained and left a deep mud puddle in the road."

"I should have been more careful."

For some reason, saying this caused her to begin crying. Slocum reached out hesitantly and put his hand on her arm. She sniffled and controlled her outburst.

"I *am* sorry, sir."

"Slocum, John Slocum," he said.

"I am so distraught. Forgive my manners. Cora Dahlquist." She thrust out a dirty hand for him to shake. He saw that she didn't have a wedding ring on her left hand but had several small silver rings on her right. He shook, then laughed.

"I'm getting you dirtier." Slocum wiped his hand on his shirt.

"Please, Mr. Slocum, come to the farmhouse with me. I promise to be quick about it."

Slocum considered what lay behind him. He doubted Turner intended to track him to the ends of the earth. More likely, he was already out on the road robbing unsuspecting pilgrims again. One drifter, no matter how many of the gang he killed, wasn't worth giving up on more unsuspecting victims passing through.

"I could use some water for me and my horse, too," he said.

Cora brightened and graced him with a smile.

"Wonderful. It's not far. Just a mile or so off the road." She pointed to a double rut leading across the prairie. By pretending, Slocum saw a farmhouse. As they got closer, his imagination worked less and his eyes more. The farm-house was in need of repair and the fields stretching out to the west had been planted but were in need of tending. Nearby rolling hills gave some character to the land. Every-thing about the place reminded him of Cora—once elegant but now turning a little shopworn.

"I hope the pump is still working." Cora made a vague motion toward the towering windmill. Its blades turned fitfully in the wind and made a grinding sound rather than one Slocum associated with pumping.

"You might need grease on the gears," he said.

"There's so much that's needed around here," she said sadly. Cora smiled weakly and said, "Let's get you out of those clothes." She clamped her mouth shut and blushed a vivid red when she realized what she had said. "I mean, dirty, wash, need—oh!"

She broke out crying again.

"You look as if you need a hand around here," Slocum said.

"I've asked around town but Mr. Goodman is doing all he can to scare off anyone wanting the job."

"The town banker," Slocum said.

"Why, yes. How'd you know?"

"We had a few words," Slocum said.

"You work for him?" Cora backed off, looking fright-ened.

"Truth is, he warned me off working here. I just didn't know what he was talking about at the time." Slocum stud-ied the farmhouse. Paint would fix it up just fine. The barn needed more work, but not that much more. The fields would take the most work, but then they always did. The wheat was close to shoulder high.

"You'd work here?"

Slocum nodded.

"I've worked in worse places, and I'm not heading any-where in particular right now." He doubted Turner would spend any time at all hunting him down. Kent was the only one of his gang who had seen Slocum, and he struck Slocum as the kind of man who wasn't too eager to seek out a fight, especially after getting shot. If Kent pretended Slocum didn't exist any longer, then he wouldn't.

"I—we—can't pay you. Nothing but room and board. When the crops are in, we can offer something then, but right now there's no spare cash."

"We?"

"My sister Laura and—" Cora jumped when a man galloped into the yard on a lathered horse. Both horse and rider had eyes that were wide and wild, but Slocum wondered if the rider frothed at the mouth, too. He had a rabid, haunted look about him.

"Cora, she's in trouble. Laura's in a world of trouble and there's nothing I can do!"

"My brother, Marcus," she said in resignation. To her brother she said, "What happened? Don't tell me that horrid Mrs. Wilson had the marshal arrest her." As an aside, Cora said to Slocum, "Mrs. Wilson runs the general store. We are a . . . a little behind in payments."

"Cowboys. Ruffians!" Marcus seemed to see Slocum for the first time. He pointed an accusing finger. "Cowboys like him!"

"What sort of trouble are you talking about?" Slocum asked. He ignored what Marcus obviously intended as an insult. Some of the finest men Slocum had ever known were cowboys, rough around the edges maybe, but honest and hardworking. There could be no insult putting him in their company.

"I don't have time to stand around palavering with the likes of you," Marcus said. "Cora, where's Papa's gun?"

"Marcus, be serious. You don't know how to shoot any more than you know how to farm."

"She's in trouble, Cora. The marshal is scared of the cowboy and isn't going to do squat. Somebody has to help her!"

"I'll see what can be done," Slocum said. He brushed off some of the caked dirt on his clothing, letting it fall away and show the Colt Navy in its cross-draw holster.

"What is he, a gunfighter?"

"Sounds like you need one about now," Slocum said.

"Please, Mr. Slocum, it's asking too much of you. Marcus and my sister and I inherited our parents' farm a month back. We don't know anything about doing chores or keeping the crops growing, but we have to try."

"Why weren't you with them? Why were you in St. Louis?"

"All three of us were sent off for schooling. Mama insisted we get decent education. She had no idea when she married Papa he would insist on homesteading . . . here."

"You pa wasn't much of a farmer, either, was he?"

"This is all we have left," Cora said.

"If we don't help Laura, it'll be just the two of us," Marcus said. He stormed into the house, slamming the door as he went. Slocum heaved a sigh, grabbed his horse's reins, and mounted.

"You stay here and keep your brother from doing anything foolish."

With that Slocum wheeled about and got his horse into a quick trot, cutting across the prairie in what had to be a more direct route to town. In his rush, he had forgotten to ask for a description of Laura Dahlquist, but he figured he wouldn't have too much trouble finding her. She'd be with a cowboy and the marshal would be at the other end of town.

He rode into Bitter Creek again, more alert this time for trouble in the town rather than on his back trail. Getting Cora's buggy free of the mud hole and the trip to the Dahlquist farm had taken several hours. It was now somewhere past noon, and to Slocum's surprise the saloon showed a considerable amount of activity. The men ought to be on their farms, working away until sundown. Maybe then they would drift into town, but seldom before when there were chores to do.

But then Marcus had said the man assaulting his sister had been a cowboy. There weren't ranches in this part of Indian Territory, so that meant she had fallen into trouble with somebody without a job.

Slocum dismounted and poked his head into the saloon but saw nothing amiss. A half dozen men, all with their backs turned to him, worked on tepid beers at the long bar. He ducked back out and looked around. He heard the ruckus before he saw what was going on. At the side of the hotel, in deep shadows, he caught signs of movement. With a long and determined stride, he crossed the street and entered the alley to get a better look.

A man held a woman's wrists in one burly fist as he forced her against the wall. His hips slammed forward repeatedly. Slocum saw he had his pants down around his ankles and the woman's skirt was bunched up around her waist. Her face was averted, but from the way she sounded, he knew what her expression would be.

Slocum took three quick steps and swung an iron fist as hard as he could. He caught the man on the side of the head and staggered him. His feet tangled in his dropped pants and he was sent crashing to the ground. From the sound of the impact it might have been a giant redwood being felled on the California coast. The man was a giant.

"You Laura?" Slocum asked.

She turned her strained white face toward him and nodded once. Slocum was taken aback. Cora was a beauty. Her sister was even lovelier, even considering what she had gone through.

Slocum didn't bother asking any more questions. The man on the ground fought to get his pants pulled up.

"Don't bother, 'less that's the way you want to be buried." Slocum drew his six-shooter in a smooth move and fired.

"Damnation!" the man cried out.

"Damnation is right," Slocum said. "I intended the slug to kill you, you miserable, raping son of a bitch." He cocked his six-gun again, wondering how he had missed at this range. Before he fired again he saw the reason leaking from the gun barrel. He was lucky the weapon hadn't blown up in his grip. He had gotten mud into the barrel while getting Cora's buggy free. The first slug had gone off target. Whether a second would do any better wasn't something he could tell without firing.

He did.

This slug missed its target, too. Both bullets had found a home in the giant of a man, but neither was fatal. Slocum had aimed both for the man's heart.

"What's got into you, you stupid little ass wart?" The man twisted around and came to his feet. "I was jist havin' me some fun."

"She wasn't having any fun."

"Didn't say she was. *I* was havin' all the fun. Took me long enough to chase her down since she got away from me a couple times." By now the man had his smoke wagon out and rolling.

Slocum and the cowboy fired at the same time. Slocum winced as lead grazed his arm. He felt the hot streak the entire length inside his left biceps and across his side as the slug managed to tear away flesh on both body parts.

For the third time, his six-shooter failed him. This time there was only a dull *pop!* He had dropped his hammer on a dud.

Slocum never let the man get off a second shot. He stepped forward and used his pistol as a club. The sound of bone crunching as metal met the man's temple told the story. This time when the cowboy went down, he went down for keeps, the side of his head all stove in.

Stepping back, Slocum considered taking the time to clean his six-gun and finish the job. The sound of horses in the street behind him convinced him there wasn't time. The man's partners had located him and were yelling.

"Come on," Slocum said, grabbing Laura by the arm. She flinched away, but he didn't release her. He half dragged her to the back of the alley and shoved her out of sight, following an instant later when he caught sight of the man coming down the alley.

Kent!

Beside the limping outlaw were two others. From the way the man on the left acted, he had to be Turner, which meant the man Slocum had just killed was another of the gang.

"Let me go!"

Slocum clamped his hand over Laura's mouth to keep her quiet. If Turner heard so much as a mouse scratching its balls, he would come to avenge the death. Slocum chanced a quick look and saw Turner and Kent hurrying back down the alley. They mounted and raced out of town, shooting as they went. He heard glass breaking and outraged citizens protesting at how the Turner Gang was hurrahing their town. They didn't realize how close they had come to having Turner commit even greater outrages on them and their town.

"You l-let her go or I swear, I'll k-kill you!"

Slocum heard the distinctive metallic click of a six-gun hammer being pulled back. He stepped to one side of Laura Dahlquist but kept his grip on her mouth to prevent her from crying out.

Slocum stared down the bore of an impossibly big six-shooter held in Marcus Dahlquist's shaking hands. One mistake and a bullet would end Slocum's life right then. Given how spooked Marcus looked, Slocum was only a hairsbreadth from dying at the hands of the brother of the woman he had just saved.

4

"Put that down!" Laura Dahlquist pushed Slocum aside and stood between him and her brother. Slocum rested his hand on her shoulder, but she shrugged it off. "You listen to me, Marcus Lane Dahlquist! He *saved* me."

"He's one of them," Marcus said, his hands shaking even more. Slocum watched the muzzle of the six-shooter trace out a huge circle. If the man shot at any point, there was no telling what he would hit. Slocum started to level his Colt Navy, but Laura grabbed his wrist and forced his hand down.

"You stay out of this," she said sharply.

"Looks like I'm the center of it. Your brother wants to kill something, and I'm all he's got."

"I won't let him," she said.

"I won't, either," Slocum said in a voice so cold it caused Marcus to take a step back and clutch the pistol with both hands.

"I'm going to kill you!"

Laura stepped forward and grabbed the six-gun. It discharged. She yelped as it burned her hand. Slocum moved like a striking snake. For two cents he would plug Marcus or buffalo him, but Laura had risked her life for him and she obviously wanted her brother alive. Slocum launched a haymaker that shook him down to his toes when his fist landed squarely in the center of Marcus's belly. The man let out a sound like a faulty blacksmith's bellows and dropped to his knees, retching weakly.

"What 'n the bloody hell's goin' on?"

Slocum and Laura turned in unison and looked back down the alley. A slat-thin man shuffled along, a shotgun preceding him.

"Y'all show yourselves now, you hear? I'm runnin' you in for killin' this deceased gent."

Slocum pulled Laura back out of sight and said, "The marshal. Let's get out of here."

She nodded and turned to face her brother.

"Get on your feet," she said sternly. "If you don't, the marshal is going to arrest you for murder."

"Didn't kill him," Marcus gasped out.

"Won't matter," Laura said.

Slocum shoved his six-shooter into its holster, got his arm around Marcus, and heaved him to his feet. The man stumbled and tried to force himself away from Slocum.

"Come on," Slocum said, making sure the man's pistol was aimed away. He hurried Marcus along, cut across a lot, and went down another alley into the street running parallel. Bitter Creek had several streets and a population of several hundred. Large enough to be noticed but not large enough to disappear in a mob.

"There's Cora!" Laura left Slocum and her brother and went to the buggy. The sisters hugged and then Laura got into the buggy. By this time Slocum had their brother in position to pick him up by collar and belt and heave him behind the two women.

"Drive," Slocum said. "Get back to the farm and don't let him poke his head up." Slocum slammed Marcus flat behind the seat.

"Thank you, John," Cora said. Her eyes flashed with anger, but it was directed at her brother. She snapped the reins, got the buggy turned around, and drove away toward the Dahlquist farm.

Slocum wended his way back through the buildings until he came out on the main street where he had left his mare. A knot of men stood at the mouth of the alley, all shouting to the marshal. Slocum mounted and rode out of Bitter Creek without attracting any unwanted attention. He hoped that Turner shooting up the town as he rode out had cemented the notion in everyone's heads that the outlaw was responsible.

When he got to the edge of town, he put his spurs to the mare's flanks and galloped off and overtook the buggy within a few minutes.

"You're responsible!" shouted Marcus. "You let him rape my sister!"

"If you don't put that six-shooter away, I'll cram it down your throat," Slocum said.

"I can protect my family, if you'll let me."

Slocum hesitated a moment, then laughed and shook his head sadly.

"How old are you? You talk like a five-year-old," Slocum said.

"You hold your tongue," Cora said, glaring at him. "He's our brother and he's trying to do his best."

Slocum considered letting the trio return to their farm and muddle through on their own. They had a peculiar way of doing things, and it wasn't his.

"I'll be taking my leave. Cora, Laura," he said, touching the brim of his hat.

"Wait, John. That's your name, isn't it? Please, John. Come back to the farm with us. I need to thank you," Laura said.

"I've been thanked good enough," he said, staring at Marcus. The man sulked now. He looked to be in his early twenties, but his behavior would have been punished by an exacting schoolmarm. Slocum saw that the two women took care of him as if each was his mother. With the six-gun he waved around, that could be a big problem if either woman wasn't there to tell him what to do—and who not to shoot.

"At least let me clean your clothes. I promised, and I'm not one to go back on my promises," Cora said.

Slocum's belly rumbled and his mouth felt like the inside of a cotton bale.

"I could use some water for my horse, too. And some feed, if you have it."

"We don't owe him anything!"

"Be quiet, Marcus," Laura said. "He saved me from being . . . taken advantage of."

Laura turned pale at the thought of what had happened to her. Slocum saw a steel core in the woman, but she was in shock over how Turner's henchman had used her. She turned and stared forward, as stiff as a board, as the buggy rattled along. Slocum rode to the turnoff to the farm and knew then he had to make a decision.

As if both he and his horse came to the same conclusion, they trotted alongside the buggy all the way into the farmhouse yard, scattering chickens and creating something of a furor among the milk cows in a pen behind the house.

"You go on into the house, Marcus," Cora said. "We'll take care of everything."

"Don't trust him. He's one of them. Look at the way he carries that six-gun! He's a gunman, just like them."

Slocum stepped down and wrapped the reins through an iron ring on a post near the house. He stayed clear of the three as they continued their argument. When Laura took her brother by the arm and half-pulled him along after her, Slocum relaxed a mite. Marcus was too wild and careless in the way he waved around his pistol. Cora came to him, eyes averted and obviously uneasy.

"I can't apologize enough for him, John. Marcus thinks he has to do everything."

"There's plenty of work to go around on a farm," Slocum said. She lifted her bright blue eyes and stared at him.

"You are a remarkable man. You understand everything."

"Where can I get that bath? Around back?"

"We have a small bathhouse behind the barn. There's a fire pit so we can heat water and bathe in relative privacy."

"I'll get on with it. There's no need for you to wash my clothes."

"But—"

"I'll need to take care of my horse," he said. "I'll do that first while the water for the bath is heating."

"I . . . I'll leave you to your ablutions," she said. A tiny smile curled her lips and she shyly reached out, touched his arm, and then rushed back to the house. Slocum sighed. She was a lovely woman but as long as she was saddled with her brother and his behavior, she wasn't going to blossom.

He pulled the reins free from the ring and led his horse to the barn. The door hung against one hinge, forcing him to lift and struggle to get it open. He found what he expected inside. The stalls had not been mucked recently and the equipment hanging on the walls sorely needed repair. He found one stall with fresh straw in it and put his mare in. After a few minutes searching, he found a canister of oats and let the horse feed while he curried and got the worst of the mud off the horse's legs.

After he had finished tending to his mare, Slocum went out back and looked around. He let out a low whistle. When Cora had said they had a bathhouse, he had thought it would be nothing more than a pile of hay bales around a galvanized tub. He had not realized she meant a real building. He poked his head inside and looked around. Flagstones had been laid around the large tub and two nearby tables were stacked with bath salts and other female scrubbing-down condiments. The bar of soap was all Slocum needed.

He found the fire pit and a stack of wood. They might let the farm fall apart but they sure enjoyed their luxuries. He pumped a large pot of water, boiled it, and then dumped it into the tub. He started a second pot heating, then went into the bathhouse and stripped off his clothes.

He sank into the tub and let the hot water ease the aches and pains he had accumulated over the past few days running from Turner's gang and dealing with Marcus Dahlquist. A small noise brought him around. He had left his clothes by the door and now they were gone. Slocum reached for his six-gun, which he always kept close at hand. He dropped the pistol back when he saw Laura in the doorway, holding the pot of water he had been heating out back.

"Cora is cleaning your clothes. It might take her a while," Laura said. She came into the bathhouse and clumsily kicked the door shut as she struggled with the water.

Slocum sank back into the water and said nothing. Their eyes locked and then Laura moved closer.

"Let me heat things up," she said.

"With the water?"

"Yes," she said, pouring in the water. Slocum sat a little straighter. The water was hot, but he wanted to hide his real reaction to seeing her come into the bathhouse. Cora was beautiful. Laura was even prettier.

She dropped the bucket and began unbuttoning her blouse.

"It is hot in here," she said.

"Getting hotter," Slocum allowed.

"Not yet, but it will," she said, stripping off her blouse and tossing it onto a table. With a shimmy, she got her undergarment down to hang around her waist. She was half naked and even lovelier than Slocum had thought. Her breasts were firm and capped with hard little coppery buttons, showing her real feelings.

"Why?" Slocum asked. "You were raped."

"I was *almost* raped," she said. "He had problems because I wasn't struggling enough to get him hard. You don't have that problem, do you?" She dropped to her knees beside the galvanized tub. Her hand vanished under the surface of the water and found his hardness, showing he had no trouble responding to her.

"Reckon not," he said. "Are you sure?"

"I owe you."

"Cleaning my clothes will be payment enough."

"Cora is tending to that. I want to thank *you*." Her hand began working up and down slowly, making Slocum squirm about and slosh water from the tub.

"You're getting your skirt wet," he said.

"That's not all that's getting wet," Laura said. She stood and unhooked her skirt, then stepped out of it. She slid down the linen bloomers so Slocum saw her entirely naked for the first time. He had no trouble at all staying hard with such a luscious sight.

"You're sure?" he asked again.

She stepped over to the tub and put one foot then the other in as she faced him. She slowly lowered herself. Reaching down, she caught him and guided his length directly to her heated core. He reached out and put his hands on her hips and began pushing and pulling her about to get more firmly seated. Then he gasped when she relaxed her legs entirely, causing him to race fully into her yielding body.

For a moment, Slocum simply sat in the hot water, relishing the feel of the woman all around him. Then he bent forward to give her even more of what he already felt. His lips curled around a nipple close to his face. He sucked hard and drew it into his mouth, using tongue and lips and teeth on the sensitive flesh. The tip had been hard before. Now he felt every pulse of her frenzied heartbeat through the nip.

He quickly abandoned this tasty treat and took in the

other. Then he slowly slid down the snowy slope to the deep valley between and kissed and lapped there until Laura shivered with desire.

"I want more, John. Give me more."

"You're in position to do it," he said. His hands left her hips and moved around to her firm, well-fleshed buttocks. Gripping tightly, he kneaded as if he had grabbed two lumps of pliant, yeasty dough. The more he tried to mold them into different shapes, the more the woman moved around him. He felt powerful contractions clamp down on his length, then relax.

"Oh, oh," she gasped out. He lifted and she cried out as he almost slid free of her tightness. Pulling on his twin handholds brought her back down around his hardness. Water sloshed out onto the flagstones but neither noticed. The heat came from within them now.

Slocum pushed and pulled, lifted, and got Laura moving in a rhythm that made him even harder within the hot, moist carnal tunnel. She put her hands on his shoulders for leverage and began moving faster, finding the right speed to give them both the release they needed. Slocum wanted it to last forever but could not hold back.

Her beauty, her skill, the feel of warm water and warmer flesh all around wore him down fast. The lava-hot flow from deep within him rose and then erupted at the same time the woman threw her head back, arched her spine, and let out a loud, long animal cry of release. Then she sank back, her arms around Slocum's neck.

He felt her hot breath against his wet skin. When her breathing settled down she rocked back.

"Something's missing," Laura said, smiling wickedly.

"That happens," Slocum said. "I usually find the trail again after a spell."

"Do tell. You are quite the explorer." Laura slid back and sat over his upper thighs so she could reach down and fumble under the water for his limp organ. She caressed and squeezed and began to resurrect him. Slocum leaned forward to kiss her when he heard movement outside the bathhouse. He recoiled and reached for his six-shooter. She caught his wrist and shook her head.

"Be quiet," she whispered. Amid loud sloshing, she stood and stepped out of the tub. She hastily dried herself with a towel he had not seen hanging from a hook in the wall and began climbing into her skirt and blouse, leaving her bloomers on the floor.

Laura blew him a quick kiss and looked out the door, slid through it, and disappeared. Seconds later, the door opened a crack and Cora called, "John, do you need more hot water?"

"I reckon so," he said, slipping down under what water remained. He and Laura had caused quite a tidal wave in the large tub with their lovemaking. Although he and Laura had not moved that energetically, most of the bathwater had sloshed out.

"Good," Cora said, coming into the bathhouse carrying the bucket of steaming water. She grinned even more broadly when she saw what her sister had worked so hard to bring back to life poking up out of the water.

She poured the water into the tub and stared down at Slocum for a moment, then began unbuttoning her blouse.

Slocum worried that she would see her sister's bloomers in a pile at the side of the tub, but she was too intent on other things.

"Are you sure this is what you want?" Slocum asked.

"I cleaned your clothes. They're drying outside on the clothesline. But that hardly seems enough reward after all you've done for us—for me." She dropped her blouse and unbuttoned her skirt to stand naked before him.

Slocum wasn't able to deny her.

5

Slocum pounded in the last nail needed to hold the fence around the garden upright and keep out marauding deer and other critters. It was a good thing he didn't need any more. There wasn't any money to buy more nails in Bitter Creek. The week he had worked on the Dahlquist farm had shown the real problem they had wasn't lack of willingness to work hard but rather a lack of money for essentials. He rested against the top rail and looked across the yard to where Laura spread feed for the chickens. The few remaining hens came up and pecked diligently, but Slocum wondered if they realized they didn't have to fight over the sparse grain the way they did even a few days earlier.

Their feathered companions had gone to feed the four humans. Soon enough, there wouldn't be enough hens left to reliably gather eggs every day. That would mean the cook pot for the rest. After that, the milk cows would be butchered—both of them. The bull would follow, no longer needed for the two milk cows. Slocum had never seen what had happened to the calves and reckoned they were either sold or eaten.

"Cora, Laura, it's gone! I can't find it anywhere!" Marcus ran up, waving his arms like the blades on the sluggishly turning windmill.

Reluctantly, Slocum gave up his respite from work—and from looking at Laura's trim shape as she bent and moved—and went to see what the current disaster was. Marcus had a way of making mountains out of molehills, but this time there was a shrill tone to his complaint that warned Slocum something important had happened.

"What's gone, Marcus?" Laura asked. She brushed back her dark hair and looked even more desirable to Slocum. She was tan and yet her cheeks kept a rosy glow. The two of them had snuck off repeatedly during the past week and found a variety of places to make love. After the first time with Cora, she had made herself a stranger in Slocum's bed, and he wondered why. The two sisters seemed to be on good terms, unlike their relationship with their ne'er-do-well brother, but that meant nothing. For all he knew, they shared their menfolk and never thought twice about it, though that hardly seemed likely from the way Cora acted. She was a bit of a prude, even if she did cut loose with him that first day.

Laura struck him as more calculating in the way she seduced him. Granted, it wasn't hard because he enjoyed their time together. She coaxed him sexually to keep him from riding on, and he was willing to trade his work for room, board—and her in his bed. It was the perfect bargain, since each got what he or she wanted most.

"The bull. The bull's gone. I put it in the east pasture and it's gone!"

Slocum pictured the small pasture in his mind. There were several places where the fence needed repair but they didn't have the money for more barbed wire to fix the spots. Slocum had done what he could by putting in extra fence posts that would force the bull to push them aside, but the animal was so huge that it wouldn't be a problem if the ton of gristle and mean took it into its head to get out.

"Did you see where the bull got free?" Slocum asked. Marcus glared at him, then pointedly turned and spoke to his sister.

"It was there this morning. I went out to bring it in and . . . it was gone."

"Was there a break in the fence?" Laura asked. "If there was and that's how the bull got out, we can track it." She looked pointedly at Slocum. Her meaning was clear enough. If the bull had broken through the fence and left a trail, *he* could track it and bring it back.

"I didn't see anything. Honest, Laura. There wasn't a hole anywhere!"

"The bull didn't sprout wings and fly," she said with barely restrained anger.

"I'll go look," Slocum cut in. "There might be another explanation."

"What?" both brother and sister said simultaneously.

"I spotted a couple riders the other night. There wasn't any reason for them to be here, but they galloped off when I went to see what they were up to."

"Rustlers? That old bull wouldn't fetch a plugged nickel. It can hardly service the two cows without passing out from exhaustion," said Marcus.

Laura and Slocum exchanged looks and kept grins off their faces. There was a considerable amount of other servicing going on that didn't have anything to do with the bull and cows.

"You fail at making the farm pay and what happens?" Slocum asked.

Laura looked away, as if some guilty thought entered her mind.

Marcus bristled and said, "That's not going to happen! We'll make it. We'll show 'em all. Papa loved this farm and we're not giving it away, no matter what!"

Their reactions answered Slocum's question more elo-
quently than a long legal description of the possibilities.
Laura wanted to sell while Marcus had his worth as a man
tied up with proving the farm. It didn't matter that he knew
next to nothing about being a farmer, and he wasn't learning fast enough to make much of a difference. Only good
rain and a considerable run of good luck would bring in the
wheat already in the fields and make it pay.

Slocum wondered who Laura intended selling the farm
to, then decided it did not matter. The banker was the most
likely buyer. He had not wanted Slocum or anyone else to
help the Dahlquists, so the price would sink after they became desperate.

"Losing the bull isn't the end of the world," Slocum
pointed out.

"Damned near," muttered Laura. She put her hand over
her mouth at such language. Her brother never noticed.

"The east pasture?" Slocum asked. Marcus nodded.

"I'll come with you," Laura said. "Two sets of eyes are
better than one."

"I can—" Marcus began. He shut up when Laura silenced him with a glare. Again Slocum saw the way they
related was more scolding mother to errant child than
brother to sister.

Slocum saddled two horses and rode toward the pasture
with Laura beside him.

When they were out of earshot, Slocum asked, "Who
wants to buy the place?"

"It's not for sale. Marcus would never allow it."

"Who do you have to buy it when he finally gives in?"

She looked at him sharply, then heaved a sigh. "You are
too clever by half, John. The bank is going to foreclose on
us if we can't make a payment at the end of the season."

Slocum told her how Goodman had tried to chase him
off when he had just ridden into Bitter Creek.

"That son of a bitch!" she cried. This time she made no

move to excuse her language. "He'll profit immensely if he takes back this farm."

"Good soil, decent water," Slocum said, nodding. A family who had grown up farming could make a success of the place. For the Dahlquists, it would be a harder row to hoe.

"You looking to sell before he can foreclose? Is that why Cora has spent so much time in town this past week?"

"That's not it, not exactly," Laura said. She pointed and cried, "There! That's where the bull got out!"

Slocum rode to the spot where a fence post lay on the ground, the wire loose around it.

"That damned bull ran up against it and knocked over the post and got out and—"

"And the bull didn't rub against the post," Slocum said. He jumped to the ground and examined both fence and wire before looking at the soft earth on the far side of the fence. "Somebody roped the post and pulled it out. There are the hoofprints." He stood and walked around to the spot where the bull's hoofprints headed out of the pasture. "They might have roped the bull and led him out."

"They?"

"Two sets of tracks, a few yards away. I can't make them out anymore since the bull is cutting up so much turf."

"Someone stole our bull!"

Slocum nodded slowly. There was no telling who might have done it. A solitary bull meant little to rustlers unless they took it for dinner. Since there weren't any steers or heifers in the pasture, the tough old bull might have looked as attractive as it got for hungry rustlers. Or it could have been someone Goodman hired, or even another farmer wanting to make life harder for the newcomers.

"Who owns the land yonder?" Slocum pointed in the direction of the tracks.

For a moment Laura didn't answer. Then she said in a voice almost too low for Slocum to hear, "Hop Franks."

"He likely to steal your bull?"

"I don't think so. He's sweet on Cora."

Slocum considered this for a moment. He took extra time to find the trail leading from the Dahlquist farm and get the direction settled in his mind before mounting again.

"That where she's been spending all her time this past week?" He couldn't forget how both women had come to him while he was in the bathhouse. He hadn't had a cleansing like that since. Without realizing it, he pressed his hand into the front of his clean shirt. Cora had done quite a job cleaning his clothes and had even ironed the shirt. Not once since he had bought the shirt in a Fort Smith store had it been pressed after cleaning.

"Yes."

Slocum saw she was reluctant to speak more, but he guessed that Cora might be engaged in a little sweet talk with the man who owned the farm adjacent to their property in an attempt to get money from him. Cora might love the man or only want to spend some time with him, but from the way Laura tried to maneuver him around, Slocum wouldn't put anything past the beautiful sisters. Not that he was complaining . . .

"Should we go after the bull?" Laura asked. "Whoever stole it is likely to be dangerous."

Slocum had spent an hour cleaning his Colt and making sure its precision mechanism was well oiled and worked perfectly. There would not be a repeat of the misfiring that had occurred back in Bitter Creek when he had taken on Turner's gunman.

"Doesn't matter. Somebody stole your bull. I'll get it back."

Laura tried to talk him out of the pursuit but Slocum pushed on. She followed reluctantly and then drew rein when Slocum stopped suddenly.

"Looks to be a case of murder," Slocum said.

"Murder? Who? The bull! Oh, no!"

Whoever had stolen the bull from the pasture had shot it.

From the number of bullet holes, it seemed they had tormented the poor animal, filling it with lead until it could no longer stand. Even then, it might have been an accident that a single bullet had entered just behind its head. Slocum had seen such wounds kill even such a huge animal instantly.

"We ought to dress it out and eat it," he said.

Laura made a strangled noise, turned, and galloped off. Slocum waited a minute longer, studying the terrain all around. Tracking the bull's killers was impossible because they had ridden to a nearby stream and had used its rapidly flowing water to hide their trail. They might have gone upstream or down. Slocum doubted it was worth the effort ranging up and then down to be sure he had the right tracks. They might also have split up, one going in each direction. He shrugged it off. Dressing out the bull was more important, but he needed help and maybe the flatbed wagon to get the meat back to the farmhouse.

He trotted after Laura and found the woman on the front porch, waving about a slip of paper. Before he could dismount, she cried, "That fool brother of mine's gone into town! He's taken it into his head that Hop Franks is responsible for all our troubles."

"He have reason to think that?"

"He's just angry that Hop is courting Cora. I didn't even have a chance to tell him about the bull."

Slocum's mind raced. He ought to ride out now. Getting involved in a family feud like this was foolhardy and could only bring woe to everyone concerned.

"Go after him, John. As a favor for me. He's going to get hurt." Laura stared at the page and then back at Slocum. "More likely, he'll get hurt bad. Hop isn't the most even-tempered man in Bitter Creek."

"Did Marcus take his pa's gun again?"

"He sleeps with it under his pillow. Since you rode in, he hasn't let it out of his sight, not even when he goes to the outhouse."

Slocum didn't blame Marcus for that. He had seen more than one man killed with his pants down, but he didn't say anything to Laura about that.

"What if he won't come back all peaceable? He's mighty wild waving that hogleg around."

"I know, I know," she said fretting. "Don't let him hurt anyone."

Slocum took her meaning. She was willing to sacrifice her brother to keep Hop Franks from getting a hole or two shot in his hide. Or maybe there was more to it. Slocum had seen how the sisters shared him, but did Cora know she had come to Slocum immediately after Laura had left? Did Laura know what had gone on when her sister had come into the bathhouse? Slocum wasn't sure he wanted to dig too deeply into that pile to find what was under it.

All the way back into Bitter Creek he thought about what he had gotten himself into when he had agreed to a simple bath to clean off some mud. The Dahlquist sisters were about the prettiest things he had ever seen. Cora had set his heart beating faster just looking at her, and Laura was even more beautiful. How two such women had a brother like Marcus was a mystery Slocum did not care to visit.

The ways of the world were too often strange.

It didn't take him long at all to find Marcus. Laura's fears were borne out by the fight going on in the middle of the town's main street. A dozen men had gathered in a ring. From Slocum's position atop his mare, he saw Marcus Dahlquist facing another man, taller, older, and with a hardness to him that foretold the winner of any real fight.

"You leave my sister alone. You just want our farm!" Marcus shouted and got jeers from the crowd as a reward. The young man's wild look silenced the crowd.

"She can make up her own mind. You're not her pa," the man Slocum took to be Hop Franks said. From the way the farmer stood with bony hands clenched and shaking just a little, he was wound up and ready to explode. Marcus either saw that and reacted or simply went off the rails.

He went for his six-shooter.

"Marcus, no!" Cora rushed forward, but Hop Franks pushed her back out of the line of fire.

"I ain't armed," Franks said. "You'd kill an unarmed man? You that kind of coward?"

"Don't taunt him, Hop. Please, don't," Cora said. She tried to grab Franks's arm but again he shoved her away.

From the way Marcus tensed, Slocum knew what was coming. He moved without giving the matter a thought. His heels raked the sides of his mare and they rocketed forward. As he raced past, Slocum got his foot out of the stirrup cup and kicked hard. The toe of his boot caught Marcus Dahlquist on the upper arm, sending him staggering. This was all it took for several of the men in the crowd to pile on. One yanked the six-gun from Marcus's hand and others pinned his arms and legs down until he looked like a mangy dog infested with fleas.

"Git on off him, now. Git!" The marshal appeared, looking around nervously. Slocum came up behind Hop Franks. This time the farmer didn't push Cora away but rather drew her in close to his body, a protective arm around her shoulders.

"He's tryin' to run us off. He's a devil!" Marcus struggled in the grasp of a pair of men. They released him when the marshal instructed them to do so.

"You been out in the sun too long?" the marshal asked, pushing his index finger into Marcus's chest. "Hop there, he ain't tryin' to do no such thing."

"I'm courting his sister, and he can't stand the notion of having me as a brother-in-law."

Slocum looked down and saw the surprise on Cora's face. The notion of marriage must not have occurred to her, or if it had, she'd never thought the farmer would agree.

Slocum snorted. Cora might be as much a fool as her brother if she believed that. There wasn't a man in Bitter Creek who wouldn't give up a wife or otherwise agree to marry a woman so lovely at the drop of a hat.

"I'm runnin' you in so you can cool off," the marshal said, dragging Marcus along. Someone handed the marshal Marcus's pistol. He tucked it in his belt as he grabbed Marcus by the collar and steered him down the street.

Marcus fought—but not good enough. The marshal drew his pistol and laid it alongside the man's head, driving him to his knees in the middle of the street.

"You try that again and I'll see you buried out on the prairie, not even a marker on your damn grave. Now come *on*." The marshal got Marcus moving while the younger man held the side of his head as he tried to stop the flow of blood from the shallow cut laid there by the six-gun's barrel.

Slocum dismounted and went to Cora. She clung to Hop Franks as if he would keep her from falling.

"You all right?" Slocum asked, ignoring Franks.

"She's right as rain. Who the hell are you?"

"You want to get on back to the farm while I see to your brother?"

"I asked you a question." Hop Franks pushed Cora behind him and balled his hands into bony fists. Standing in front of the farmer, Slocum saw that those fists were about the size of quart jars. A punch, lucky or accurate, would knock him down. If he crossed Franks, it would have to be with a six-shooter in his hand. Fisticuffs were likely out of the question.

"I work for the Dahlquists," Slocum said. "Cora, you want to—"

"No! I'm not going back." She looked up at Franks. "Did you mean that, what you said?"

"I'd marry you in a heartbeat," the farmer said earnestly.

"Then I'm going with Hop. You can tell Laura that. I'm

sick of working my fingers to the bone, and for what? The farm is going to fail."

"What about your brother?"

"Let him rot in jail," snapped Franks.

"He . . . he's not always responsible for what he says. Marcus can be a hothead, but maybe it'll do him some good to spend a few days in jail for disturbing the peace." Cora struggled to find the reasons to leave her brother and go with Hop then and there.

"I'll press charges. He threatened to kill me," Franks said.

"Please, Hop, don't do that." Cora pulled him down and whispered to him for several seconds. Slocum saw the anger melt from the farmer like snow in the bright spring sun.

"I won't press the matter, but if he comes at me again with that gun of his, I won't be responsible for what happens. I swear, I'll cram it sideways all the way up his ass!"

Cora and Hop Franks went off, arms around each other. Slocum shook his head as they climbed into a wagon already loaded with supplies and rattled off. He watched until they were out of sight. Then he went to the jail to see what it would take to free Marcus from custody. Laura needed help doing the farm chores, and Slocum was damned if he was going to do them all by himself.

6

"It's not fair," Marcus Dahlquist groused. He rode with his shoulders slumped and eyes down. Even his horse reflected his dejection with its plodding stride.

"You getting arrested for threatening Franks?" Slocum asked. "Looks to me like the marshal was mighty accommodating, letting you go free without even a fine."

"He's in cahoots with the banker. Goodman wants our farm and the marshal will get to serve the papers and foreclose. He wants that so bad he can taste it. Keeping me in jail's nothing compared with lording it over me when he throws me off the farm."

"Why should he hate you?" Slocum couldn't care less why the marshal—or anyone in Bitter Creek—wanted to see Marcus fail. He had heard similar sentiments from other men, and it all boiled down to personal failure rather than any concerted effort against them. Still, there might be some animosity driving the townspeople, given the way Marcus Dahlquist waved that six-shooter around.

"Goodman wants the farm," Marcus said. "And he hated my pa. I don't know why."

"Sell it to him," Slocum said. "You're not cut out to be a farmer, and neither are your sisters."

"You leave them out of this!" Marcus flared. "You don't say a word against them. Either of them."

"Cora went with Hop Franks," Slocum said. "Sounded as if he might have proposed marriage to her and she accepted." He watched the young man's reaction. It was about what Slocum expected.

Marcus bolted upright in the saddle and twisted around to face Slocum so fast he almost fell off the horse.

"What the hell are you sayin'?"

"Franks has the look of a real farmer about him. His farm adjoins yours, doesn't it?"

"That's why he's courting Cora. No other reason."

Slocum snorted and shook his head. Marcus must be daft if he thought that was the only reason a lonely farmer in the middle of the Indian Territory would court his sister.

"How's he doing? Is he going to bring in a decent crop this year?"

"He's hard up for money. We all are."

"Might be you can combine your two farms and make a little less but keep both going. There'd be four of you working a larger field but that changes your chance for making it, at least this year."

"Throw in with him? Never!"

"Is that your brain or your wounded pride talking? He would have beaten the shit out of you if you'd taken him on bare knuckles."

"I can't let him marry Cora. He . . . he . . ." Marcus sputtered for words.

"He's a no-account lowlife snake in the grass?" Slocum suggested.

"Yeah, that."

"And he's a farmer, so he's beneath you. He scrabbles in the dirt and raises his own food and makes his farm succeed. You're too much of a St. Louis socialite to ever let your sister marry him."

"He's not of our social strata."

"I don't have any idea what you mean," Slocum said. "He's better than you because he works and earns his living. You hardly work and your farm is failing."

"Why don't you just ride on, Slocum? Oh, yeah, I forgot. You and Laura are—" Marcus turned pale when he saw the fire in Slocum's green eyes.

"I'm trying to help you. Take what I say with a grain of salt or listen to it. It doesn't much matter to me."

"You think he'd do that? Hop Franks?"

"Ask." Slocum rode the rest of the way back to the farm in silence, letting Marcus stew over everything Slocum had said. Slocum worried a mite that Marcus knew what was going on between him and Laura, since the man was prone to waving around his six-gun. But he must have known for a few days, and he hadn't yet tried to shoot Slocum while he slept. The way Marcus flew off the handle so easily, he was as likely to have shot both Slocum and Laura while they were together.

"Marcus, you're back!" Laura ran from the house and hugged her brother. She looked over Marcus's shoulder at Slocum and gave him a broad wink that promised so much. Slocum shifted uneasily in the saddle, thinking about what his reward was likely to be that night, and all for talking the marshal out of locking up Laura's brother.

He took Marcus's horse and led it to the barn. Slocum spent close to an hour tending the horses, not hurrying, giving Laura and Marcus plenty of time to talk over their problems. Only after he had added a new layer of saddle soap to his saddle did he saunter to the farmhouse.

Laura and Marcus sat on the porch, their heads close together, talking earnestly. Slocum considered returning to the barn when Laura motioned for him to join them.

"John, Marcus has a wonderful idea."

"Do tell." Slocum knew what it was. He listened as Laura related the idea of throwing in with Hop Franks and trying to bring in a decent crop rather than both farms struggling along and neither prospering.

"Since Cora seems to have her cap set for Hop, it makes sense to do this," she finished.

"It's your farm."

"It's Marcus's, actually. Women can't own real estate," Laura said with a touch of bitterness. Slocum wondered how the matter would have been resolved if either Cora or Laura had been able to sign the deed to the family farm.

"So, are you going to ride on over and discuss the idea? Do you think he's settled down after Marcus braced him in town the way he did?"

"There's a barn dance tonight. That might be a better time to approach him. He and Cora will have worked out the details of their nuptials, and he ought to be feeling cordial toward the Dahlquist family." Laura turned and sternly said to Marcus, "You will be polite and you will leave that horrible pistol here tonight. Do you understand me?"

"Do you think he'll agree? We got water on our property he could use, and he's got a bull. We need that or our milk cows will go dry."

"Who do you think killed your bull?" Slocum asked.

"You saw tracks of two riders. You're sure both were responsible for the slaughter?"

Slocum nodded.

"Hop lives alone. He doesn't even have a hand to help him in the fields. That's another reason why I believe combining our efforts will appeal to him."

"Looks to me that he's got Cora to help him out now."

"Oh, she won't stay there. She must come back here every night," Laura said, as if she were the sole arbiter of her sister's morals. "After the wedding, of course, she and Hop can live on his place or here, I suppose. We have an extra room."

"Not here!" Marcus's temper flared again.

Slocum slipped away to let them continue their argument. Every time he thought Marcus had some sense pounded into his head and knew where he was going, he took a different fork in the road. After finishing what chores he could, Slocum flopped into the straw in a stall, reflecting on how different the barn was after only a week. He needed to add some paint to keep the wood from rotting away, but the stalls were repaired and the entire barn cleaned out. He felt good about the work he had done—and he began wondering if it would be so bad settling down with Laura. She was a real wildcat, and a beautiful one, to boot.

He sat up when he heard the barn door creaking open. It needed oil, but right now it gave him a few seconds to see who was coming his way.

"John? There you are." Laura came and flung herself alongside him in the clean straw. "You're such a dear, giving Marcus the idea of joining our farm with Hop's."

"How'd you figure it was my idea?"

Laura laughed. "Marcus never had such a thought in his life. He thinks he will be seen as less manly if he gives up on the farm. Maybe he's right." She put her hands under her head and stared up at the ceiling where exposed nails protruded and beams sagged. The decay didn't catch her notice.

"What's in this for you?" Slocum asked. "Marcus needs to keep the farm going to prove he's the equal of his pa. Cora has Hop Franks all roped and hog-tied. Why do you stay?"

"They're family," Laura said. "There's nothing else, is there?"

Slocum considered his own restless drifting through the West and wondered. He had gotten accustomed to the distant horizon being his destination, living off the land and only taking a job when he needed gear or ammunition or something else he would be hard pressed to make for himself. Towns had their attraction—whiskey, women, cowboys who didn't know the odds at poker. But he was always glad to be in the saddle and riding for somewhere else, and it never mattered where that somewhere might be.

Now he wasn't so sure he wanted to go on without Laura beside him.

"Be ready to go to the square dance. If we leave at six we can be there before seven. That's when things get going." She rolled over, gave him a quick kiss that lingered on his lips, and then was gone.

Slocum flopped back, duplicating her pose, but he doubted he was thinking of what she had been. After a spell, he rose, heated some water, and had himself a bath. He even used some of the lavender scent in the bathwater, hoping it didn't cause him to be the object of affection by boars and bulls.

Laura gripped his arm as if he might run away. On the other side a gussied-up Marcus Dahlquist looked as uncomfortable as Slocum felt. There were too many people in the barn for comfort. Dozens of men circled endlessly, vying for the attention of the few single women in Bitter Creek. In that regard, Slocum had the jump on them all. He had the prettiest filly in all Indian Territory on his arm—and across the barn he saw the second prettiest, sitting with Hop Franks. Cora whispered endlessly in the man's ear. Slocum tried to read Hop's expression but couldn't. Cora might be telling him it looked like rain, that she wasn't wearing bloomers, or that he was the finest man who ever walked the earth.

"He's difficult to read, isn't he?" Laura said, seeing Slocum's attention directed toward Hop and her sister.

"Wouldn't want to play poker with him," Slocum allowed.

"Let's dance," Laura said, tugging insistently on his arm. "You do dance, don't you? It would be ever so much fun teaching you."

"There's nothing you have to teach me," Slocum said.

Laura smiled broadly and said, "I've noticed that."

They joined the dancers, went into a Texas star, and

were soon swinging this way and that. Slocum caught glimpses of Cora, Hop, and Marcus at first and then lost track as he got into the spirit of the dance. Laura was an armful, and moved along as if she were a thistle floating on the evening breeze.

After the dance, Slocum was a little winded.

"You surprised me, John. I didn't know you were such a fine dancer."

"I have some hidden talents."

She looked boldly at his crotch. "Perhaps they won't have to remain hidden all night long."

Before Slocum could answer, the banker came up, turned halfway toward Laura, and then shouldered Slocum to one side to face the woman squarely.

"You have a chance to talk with your lazy brother about selling?"

"You've got a strange way of buttering up someone whose land you want to buy," Slocum said from behind Goodman.

"I'm not talking to a hired hand," Goodman said without looking at Slocum. "Miss Dahlquist, my offer expires at midnight. If you wish to take it—and it is a generous offer, considering the condition of that farm—let me know. Trust me, I will not renew the offer, not even when the bank opens on Monday morning."

"Then you won't be waiting for an answer that will never be given, sir," she said sharply. Laura held out her arm to Slocum. "I feel the need to dance away my anger."

Slocum felt Goodman's eyes boring into his back as he and Laura began another dance. The fiddle player was off-key and screechy and the caller muffed the call more than once, but Slocum didn't care. Having his arm around Laura's waist, feeling her press close and then swing away, only to return, was more than enough for him.

"I am in need of some air, John. Let's go outside so I can cool off."

"Don't go cooling off too much," Slocum said as he steered her through the gathering throng of people from town. More than a hundred souls crowded into the barn, causing the already humid night to seem oppressive inside.

"My, aren't you the witty one." Laura laughed and pressed her cheek to his upper arm as they stepped out. Several other couples had the same idea. Slocum and Laura strolled along, letting the weak breeze cool them a mite.

"What did Goodman offer for the farm?" Slocum asked.

"Not enough. He knows two women and a foolish man whose idea of farming is to read about it in a novel cannot drive much of a bargain. If Papa had left it in better condition we would have had a better bargaining chip."

"How'd they die?"

"Nobody seems to know. Might have been the flu or something else. They both died within days of each other. Cora and I hurried down when we heard, but they had been buried a   nth before we arrived. It was a good thing Marcus was already on his way. He was here within days of their deaths."

"That's why the farm is in such sorry shape. You can't let weeds grow in a field for a month."

"I'm afraid you are right," she said. "For Marcus's sake, Cora and I had hoped to make a success of it and then return to St. Louis in the fall after the crop had been harvested. It doesn't look as if that is going to happen."

"You can always return," Slocum said.

"There's nothing for me there. The three of us together, well, we had fun and somehow managed to survive on the allowance Papa sent every month."

"Cora has herself a man."

"Do I, also?" Laura stared up into Slocum's eyes. As he bent to kiss her, Marcus called out to them.

"I'm going to do it. I really am. What's there to lose?"

Laura and Slocum parted somewhat guiltily. It wasn't

proper for such a display in public or even just in front of her brother.

"You're going to see if Hop wants to tear down the fence between our places?" Laura asked. "I knew you'd see your way to such a good decision." She hugged her brother and then stepped away. "Well, what are you waiting for? Go find him and ask."

"I haven't seen him."

Slocum cleared his throat and said, "Hop and your sister were out back. You might wait a while before asking him."

"No, I've got to do it now or I'll lose my nerve," Marcus said. He went away, mumbling to himself.

"I don't know what to do with him, John," Laura said. "He doesn't understand even the simpler things."

"Maybe he needs a good woman."

"Like Hop has?" Laura's question carried just a hint of steel edge to it, making Slocum wonder if she knew about him and Cora when he had first come to their farm.

"Like you," he said. This softened her mood a bit. She clung to his arm and pressed closer.

"You're such a liar, but I love it. Lie to me some more."

Before Slocum could say a word, a gunshot rang out. His hand went for the handle of his Colt Navy, then he remembered he had left the pistol and gun belt in his saddlebags. Nobody else at the dance had come with irons on their hip, so he had removed his own.

He shook off Laura's grip and ran to his mare, fumbled in the saddlebags, and whipped out his Colt Navy. From the way the crowd congregated at the rear of the barn, he knew the shot had been fired out back. Rather than push his way through those inside, he ran around the barn and skidded to a halt when he saw Marcus standing numbly, staring down at a body.

Hop Franks lay sprawled on the ground, facedown. From the way blood spread in the middle of his shirt, Slocum could tell he had been shot in the back.

7

"Where's Cora? Cora!" Laura pushed past Slocum to search for her sister. Slocum remained by Franks's body and checked to be sure the man was dead. The bullet had driven into his spine smack in the middle of his back, killing him instantly. Rolling him over, Slocum saw that the bullet had gone clean through the body.

"He . . . he's dead," Marcus said.

Slocum stood and grabbed the man's wrists and lifted his hands.

"You have that six-gun you're always waving around?"

"N-no. I've never seen a dead man before. He was murdered."

"Shot in the back. If you didn't shoot him, did you see who did?"

"Me? Kill him? No!" Marcus jerked free and stumbled away from Slocum. "I was going to make a deal with him. Why'd I want to kill him?"

"Maybe he said no. He'd have all the claim to the land that he needed by marrying Cora."

"I never said a word to him. He didn't turn me down. I

never said a word!" Marcus's voice turned so shrill Slocum felt the urge to clap his hands over his ears to shut off the whining. Even better, a short jab to Marcus's chin would not only stop the whining but would make Slocum feel better.

"Move aside, move aside, lemme in," came the marshal's irascible voice. The rail-thin man stopped and stared at Franks's body. "Son of a bitch," he muttered. "Who kilt poor ole Hop?" The marshal looked around at the gathered crowd, but his eyes stopped on Marcus Dahlquist.

"He was on his way to talk to Franks," Slocum said, "but this is what he found." He pointed to the body to get the marshal looking away from Marcus and concentrating once more on the crime.

"Why'd he want to talk to Hop? Heard tell Hop was sweet on his sister. From what I seen, Dahlquist ain't too happy when any stud comes sniffin' 'round his sisters."

"He doesn't have a gun, Marshal," Slocum said. "Look at him. Do you think he has the aspect of a man who's just gunned down another man?"

"Hell, he ain't got a spine. He'd shoot a man in the back." The marshal poked a toe into Franks's unmoving side. "Looks like a backshooter to me. Bullet hit him in the back and came tearin' out his chest." The marshal spat and shook his head. "Ugly way to die, but it was quick. Not much more a man could want."

"You thinking on checking for guns in the crowd?" Slocum looked around to see if any of the onlookers tried to sneak off. Everyone stood their ground. It had been worth a try, but whoever had killed Hop Franks had probably hightailed it. There wasn't much reason to stay and watch everyone making chin music about who might have pulled the trigger.

"Looks like a good-sized bullet ripped through him. Might be a .44 or a .45."

"That includes most folks in Bitter Creek," Slocum said.

"What's that piece you're carryin', Slocum?"

Slocum handed his Colt to the marshal. The lawman looked at the muzzle, matched it to the hole in the dead man's back, sniffed the gun, and handed it back.

"You ain't had the time to clean and oil your six-shooter," the marshal said. "Ain't been fired since the last time you oiled it, neither."

"It's a .36. You said it was a bigger slug that killed Franks."

"I did." The marshal didn't bother asking around the crowd. "We got ourselves a bad bunch in town, down at the saloon gettin' theyselves all liquored up. Might be one of them wandered up here lookin' fer tail."

Slocum stepped away and saw Laura with Cora. What the lawman said had the ring of truth to it. Franks might have objected to a drunk insulting Cora and gotten shot for his trouble. He let the lawman continue musing about what might have happened and joined the two sisters.

"Who shot him?" Slocum asked. Cora gasped, turned, and clung to her sister. Laura gave him a dark look. "The marshal is likely to figure your brother did the deed if you didn't see someone else kill Hop."

"We were out here. Kissing, necking. Hop said something, but I wasn't paying any attention because, well, I wasn't. He stood and then someone fired at us. Hop died protecting me."

Slocum spun Cora around and looked at her dress. There wasn't a speck of blood. Cora was either lying or was too shaken by seeing her husband-to-be gunned down to tell a straight story. Another explanation crossed Slocum's mind. She might be building Franks up in her own mind, him saving her. That gave a reason for what otherwise seemed to be a senseless killing.

"This the little lady what was gonna marry Hop?" The marshal elbowed Slocum out of the way and gave Cora a once-over. Slocum didn't like the leer on the lawman's lips, but when he didn't say anything more, Slocum let the matter drop.

"The saloon where the varmints gather's where I'm headin' right now. You want to come along, Slocum?"

"Why not." Slocum let the marshal lead the way. He noticed no one else from the barn dance accompanied them. Lengthening his stride to keep up, Slocum reached the saloon doors as the marshal bulled his way into the smoky interior.

"Which of you mangy prairie dogs upped and shot a man in the back just a few minutes ago?"

Slocum wasn't sure interrogation like this would accomplish what the marshal intended. Looking over the lawman's shoulder to the bar, Slocum went cold inside. He recognized Turner right away. The outlaw leader had never seen him, but Kent had. Slocum stayed in the shadows outside until he could find Kent and be sure the man wouldn't identify him and start blazing away.

"Well, howdy, Marshal. Why don't you get that scrawny ass of yours on over here and have a drink? It's on me," Turner said. He rapped on the bar with his knuckles. The barkeep jumped like someone had stuck his tail in a wringer, and put a full bottle of whiskey in front of the outlaw.

"I ain't drinkin' with the likes of you, Monty Turner," the marshal said. "If I had a Wanted poster on you, I'd run you in."

"For what?"

"Bein'. Jist bein' is good enough reason to lock you up. You and these reprobates you call a gang."

"I don't call them a gang. Why, Marshal, these cultured gentlemen are my associates."

This produced a round of laughter. Several of the men with Turner knocked back their shots of whiskey, then turned so their hands were free and ready to go for their six-shooters. Slocum saw big trouble brewing, even if the marshal thought he was immune.

And he still hadn't seen Kent. Going to the lawman's aid might set off a fight, but if Kent spotted and recognized Slocum as the one who had killed Harsch, there would be more than fists flying.

"You got the look of a man who thinks I did something against the law. What's eating you, Marshal?"

"A fine, upstandin' citizen was shot down at the barn dance."

"Now why would you think I know anything about that?" Turner asked.

"Because Hop Franks was shot in the back. You were the first one I thought of who'd do a cowardly thing like that!"

Slocum slid his six-gun from its holster but did not enter the saloon. He saw Kent come from a back room, a soiled dove trailing him. The outlaw strapped on his six-gun and stood beside his boss.

"Did he jist call you a backshooter?"

Turner didn't answer Kent. Instead Turner half turned, then unleashed a circular punch that caught the marshal squarely in the face. Nose broken and blood spurting everywhere, the lawman stumbled back and fell over a table. Turner took another drink, then slowly walked to where the marshal sat on the floor, trying to keep his broken nose from gushing even more of his life's blood.

"You might as well have said something bad about my ma," Turner said. "Calling me a name like that's not something I cotton much to." The outlaw reared back and kicked the marshal in the chest, knocking him flat to the floor. Then he proceeded to stomp the living daylights out of the man.

Slocum started into the saloon, then saw that Kent and the rest of the gang—five others he counted, though more might have been out of his line of sight—all drew their pistols and waited. If he had rushed in the way the marshal had, he would have a dozen bullets in him before he could get off a second shot.

His first instinct to kill the marshal's tormentor might be enough to freeze the others, if only for a moment. That might let him get off a couple more shots. At best he could take out three of the road agents before they killed him. Hating it, Slocum slipped back into the darkness as Turner started swearing a blue streak about getting blood on his boots from kicking the marshal.

"Get him out of here. No need to be delicate about it, boys." Turner aimed one last kick at the barely conscious marshal as Kent and another outlaw grabbed the man's arms and dragged him from the saloon.

"One, two, heave!" They tossed the marshal facedown into the street.

Kent hesitated and looked around, his hand on his six-shooter, but he didn't follow up on what was a good instinct. Slocum was standing at the edge of the building, watching. If Kent had taken a shot in his direction, the other outlaws would have found him in no time since Slocum had nowhere to run.

"Drinks are on me," Kent said, slapping his partner on the shoulder.

"You cheap son of a bitch. The drinks are on the house. You ain't never stood for a round of drinks in your life."

Arguing amiably, the two outlaws went back into the saloon. Slocum waited a moment, then stepped out to help the marshal. To his surprise, the lawman was nowhere to be seen. He looked around, but the marshal had disappeared as if he were made out of smoke. Slocum hurried down the street. He didn't have to follow the blood trail to know the marshal made a beeline for his office.

He went into the office, only to have the marshal lift a six-shooter in a shaky hand. He dropped it when he saw Slocum in the doorway.

"You were a hell of a lot of help," the lawman said.

"Sorry. I didn't want to end up with a pound of lead in my gut."

"They would have shot you from behind. That's their way."

"You know Turner?"

"Heard of him. Seen him more'n once when I was a deputy over in Fort Smith. But no way am I crossin' him. Bitter Creek ain't worth it." The marshal grimaced as he twisted around and clutched his side.

"You probably have a broken rib or two," Slocum said. "Is there a doctor to be found?"

"Ain't got one. The town's barber does what he can. Always goin' on about how barbers used to be better'n doctors in England. Never understood a word of that. He can't even give a shave without drawin' blood." The marshal gasped and sank into his chair, clutching his side.

"I'll ask at the dance."

"You do that, Slocum. You do that."

Slocum hurried back to the dance but most of the townspeople had gone home. Hop Franks's body hadn't been touched since the marshal left, except by flies coming to feast.

"Hey," Slocum called to a man putting a fiddle into a case before leaving. "You see the Dahlquists?"

"That lout Marcus and his two purty sisters? They left 'bout when you did. Reckon they was headin' on back to their farm. Surely is a shame about Hop. He was a good man. A hothead, but a good man at his core."

"Who'd want to kill him?"

Slocum might as well have given the man a hotfoot. He jumped, clutched his fiddle case to his body, and backed away.

"Hop didn't go in for makin' friends, but he was a decent farmer and a good man. Yes, sir, a good man." By this time, the fiddler had reached the side door and bolted through it, leaving Slocum alone in the empty barn. Where earlier the caller had bellowed out his crazy directions and three men had furnished the music on their fiddles and harmonicas, now only silence remained. Slocum poked about and found some liniment in a box near the back of the barn and some wrap intended for a horse's hoof. It wasn't much but would go a ways toward relieving the marshal's pain. If there were broken ribs, he would be out of action for a while.

Slocum wasn't sure what that meant to Bitter Creek, not having a marshal on the streets.

He returned to the marshal's office and wasn't too surprised to find the place stripped bare of the man's belongings. The lawman hadn't wasted any time packing his gear and getting the hell out of town. Slocum couldn't blame him too much, but it left the town in a sorry condition and vulnerable to the Turner Gang.

Slocum pulled down a shotgun from a wall rack, stuck a box of shells into his coat pocket, then loaded the scattergun. He was no peace officer and had no intention of trying to arrest Monty Turner. The owlhoot had to be put in his place, though, and nobody was left to do it.

The raucous cries from the saloon had died down, but Slocum heard familiar voices. He might take out one or two of them with the shotgun and then get to work with his sixshooter. Facing at least six men and maybe more didn't give him good odds, but Slocum was in jeopardy every minute the road agents were in town.

Barely had he gotten halfway to the saloon when the front doors slammed open and Monty Turner came out into the starlit street, bellowing at the top of his lungs.

"You sons of bitches, listen up! I own this town now. I don't even know what the hell the name of this piss hole is, and it doesn't matter. Monty Turner *owns* this here town!"

He started shooting wildly. Slocum guessed that the outlaw leader had put away too many drinks to even see clearly, but the others in his gang started spraying lead about, too. He moved back to get out of the way of any stray bullet. They were more intent on shooting up the town and scaring people than they were on killing anyone.

"Fetch them horses. We can't give 'em a good lesson, standin' here in front of a saloon. We got to show 'em we mean business!"

Two men rushed off to get the outlaws' horses. Slocum considered his chances. Five men remained: Turner and four of his henchmen. This presented him with the best chance he was likely to get of evening the odds. As he stepped into the street, he heard a gasp from off to his left. A quick look revealed Kent, bringing along three horses.

"You! You were in our camp. You gunned down Harsch!"

The other outlaws were busy emptying their guns into plate-glass windows and doors. Slocum knew if he used the shotgun, the sound would alert the road agents that somebody else had been shuffled into the deck. Dropping the scattergun, he slapped leather and got his Colt out. His first shot went wild since he was firing across his own body. He pivoted, got his feet planted, and fired again. This shot hit Kent, but the outlaw didn't go down. Instead, he dropped the horses' reins and went for his own six-gun.

In a flash, the two were exchanging shots. None of Slocum's subsequent rounds came close. Luckily, Kent was both het up and frightened, and his bullets sang all around Slocum, as if they were bouncing off an invisible barrier in front of him.

It would take only a few seconds before the rest of the outlaw gang realized what was going on. Slocum couldn't have Kent calling out for help any more than he could let him center a round on his head. When skill failed, Slocum relied on boldness. He started walking at a steady pace toward Kent. With his Colt held at arm's length he worked to get a good target.

Kent screeched and fired until his pistol came up empty. Slocum kept walking toward him until he got close enough to be sure of his target. He fired. A dark spot blossomed on Kent's forehead. He fell backward like a tree sawed down by a lumberjack. Slocum fired another time but the hammer fell on an empty chamber. Only then did he realize how close he had come to being the one dead on the ground.

"Get them horses over here, Kent, you lazy jackass."

Slocum tucked his pistol back into his holster, eyed where the shotgun had been discarded, and made a few quick estimates. He could never reach the shotgun before Turner and the others realized he wasn't Kent. Not having time to reload made turning tail and running the only logical thing.

But if he did that, the outlaws would know someone had killed one of their gang and they would come after him.

Slocum scooped up the reins and moved so he was between two of the horses. The third trailed behind.

"Here," he said, keeping his head down and hoping the outlaws were too liquored up to see straight. All it took was one to realize he wasn't Kent.

His luck held. They took the reins and moved his shields away. He turned at the last instant, bent low, and grabbed for the reins of the trailing horse. This gave the others time to mount and start their shouting and shooting rampage through town.

Slocum swung into the saddle, judged where the others went, and trailed them until one turned around in the saddle and called, "Come on, Kent. Yer missin' all the fun."

Slocum threw up his hands, let the horse bolt under him, then kicked free of the stirrups and fell heavily into the street. For a moment, the fall stunned him, but he forced himself to his feet and staggered around, cursing just loud enough to let the outlaw know he wasn't hurt. He was rewarded with loud laughter and, "You kin walk on back to camp, you sorry drunk. I told you that you couldn't hold your whiskey!"

The sound of receding hoofbeats told Slocum he had bluffed his way to safety.

He dusted himself off and went to find his mare. He had come to a decision somewhere between hitting the ground and realizing he had bluffed his way out of getting killed. After he picked up the rest of his gear at the farm, he would head westward.

8

Slocum rode to the barn and dismounted, hoping he could
get his gear and clear out before anyone noticed. He opened
the barn door and faced Laura Dahlquist. She sat on an
empty nail keg and looked up immediately.

"I wondered if you would be back. I figured you'd want
to get your belongings." She pointed to a stack. "I rolled it
all up in your spare blanket. Is that all right?"

"You don't mind if I go?" Slocum stared at her in disbelief.

"Of course, I mind! I want you to stay, but there's no
way to keep you now. Not after Hop was killed."

"What do you mean?"

"I know you're scared, John. That could happen to you,
just like it happened to Hop. Why take that chance?"

"I'm not scared," he said. He closed the barn door behind him to keep the light from a kerosene lamp next to
Laura from spilling out and drawing unwanted attention
from Cora or Marcus back in the farmhouse.

"There's no need to lie. It has to be a shock, what happened in town tonight. I heard as we rode out that the marshal ran afoul of some outlaws."

"He left Bitter Creek," Slocum said. Laura only nodded. "I went after the outlaws. There were too many of them for me to do anything, but I killed one."

"One," she said, as if this made a difference. "They'll be after you for certain now."

"They never got a look at my face."

"I just wanted to wish you blue skies and open roads." Laura stood to go. Slocum caught her by the arm and stopped her.

He saw a flash of calculation in those bright blue eyes of hers but knew she had already accomplished what she'd set out to do. Her words stung. He was no coward but it had to look that way. Worse, Slocum wondered if there might not be a touch of truth there. Running away was easier than staying and fighting.

"What am I staying for?" he asked.

"You have to ask?" She turned to him and began unbuttoning her blouse.

"Why aren't there more eggs?" Marcus demanded. He pounded his fist so hard on the breakfast table it caused the glasses filled with water to bounce. Slocum looked at him hard, but Marcus never noticed. He was too busy with his rant. "And the toast. You burned it. You know I don't like it burned."

"Fix it yourself, then," Laura said. "I'm not a good cook. You know that. And the chickens haven't been laying. It might just be the rooster." She glared at her brother, but Marcus ignored her since he was so lost in his own anger.

"You don't know what you're talking about. You're not tending them properly. Isn't that so, Slocum?"

"The rooster's been threatened with being turned into dumplings. There's not a whole lot you can do about him." He looked at Cora, who sat with her hands folded in her lap and eyes downcast. "Sometimes, a person just gets worn out."

At this she looked up at him. Her eyes were dull but clear. She might be depressed but she hadn't been crying the night away over her lost Hop Franks.

"What are we going to do?" Laura asked.

Slocum wasn't sure where she directed the question.

"We don't have any money, so we're not going to waste it, are we?" Marcus laughed harshly at this. "We have to fend off the banker at every turn because he wants to steal the place." He jumped up so fast he knocked over the chair and started spinning in a circle, laughing uproariously. "If he tries to steal the farm, he's not gonna get much. He's gonna steal . . . nothing!"

"Sit down, Marcus. Your behavior is inexcusable."

"Mine?" Marcus flared. "What about yours? You and this drifter share a bed, don't you? What do you have to say about that, Laura? What would Papa say about you and Slocum?"

"He wouldn't say a word because he's dead, Marcus. Dead!" Laura stormed from the kitchen. Marcus followed, shouting at her. Slocum rocked back in his chair and saw that Cora was studying him like he was some kind of bug crawling over her arm.

"She's why you stay, isn't she, John?"

"I considered riding on, but she convinced me to stay until you get the crop in."

"Without Hop's farm and crops, we're not going to make it. We need to sell the place before the crop's ready, so we can make the place seem better than it is."

"It is a good farm. You have sweet water. Not like the creek near town that's filled with alkali. The earth's rich. All it will take to make this place produce crops is hard work. Too bad none of you had seen a farm until after your parents died."

Cora looked away as she said, "Marcus had come here a

time or two. Fact is, he was on his way back to St. Louis when word of our parents dying reached him."

"Flu, I think he said."

"I suppose. By the time Laura and I got here, they had been buried. Those are their graves out on the hillside north of here. They can watch the sunrises and sunsets from there. Do you think anyone would mind if I buried Hop there, too?"

"Your brother might. He's got a bug up his ass lately."

"He's not like he was," Cora said. She shrugged as if the matter had settled itself in her mind. "He wouldn't like it. I suppose it's best to bury Hop in town. It's not like he was part of the family, after all. We hadn't got hitched, just . . ."

"Would you agree to selling the farm?" When she nodded, Slocum went on. "Would Laura?"

"She would. Maybe not Marcus, but we could convince him if the price was good enough."

Slocum finished the sparse breakfast and went directly to the barn to saddle his mare for the ride into town. Either he did something about selling the Dahlquist farm or he would ignore the promise he had made to Laura the night before and leave. Marcus Dahlquist was getting to be too crazy to bear. Slocum had rummaged through the rolltop desk in the parlor and found the six-shooter the man waved around so wildly and had unloaded it. But that was only a little margin of safety because Marcus might actually think to check the load.

At least Slocum had convinced himself the pistol had not been fired recently. It still stuck in his craw that Hop Franks had been cut down when Marcus was so close by, but his pa's six-shooter had been here at the farm.

He had sat at the desk and begun rifling through the papers to get a better idea about the farm and what it might be worth. When he was satisfied, Slocum set out to ride into town and do some down and dirty dickering.

* * *

"The farm isn't worth that much, Mr. Slocum." Goodman sat back, arms crossed over his chest, and glared at him. Slocum smiled and tried to keep from laughing. Goodman was a terrible liar.

"Do you play poker?" Slocum asked. He wished the banker did, because he could clean out the man within a few hands. A small tic under his left eye revealed every thought going on in the man's head, even if the way he sat, with those arms crossed tightly, did not.

"That's got nothing to do with the Dahlquist farm."

"Perhaps not," Slocum said, "but I like to think in terms of hands. The farm is on rich land, with good water."

"Next you'll tell me your winning hand is a king and a pair of queens."

"More like a pair of queens and a joker," Slocum said. "Marcus can be talked into selling, but it won't be easy. The women want to return home to St. Louis."

"A shame about their parents. I never had much dealing with them, not after I granted the loan to buy the farm, but the way they died so suddenly was a crying shame. It has to make the ladies want to get away from the farm and back to somewhere they can feel . . . at home."

Slocum let the banker ramble on, convincing himself he was driving the deal. After another twenty minutes, Goodman had offered more than Slocum would have thought the farm was worth—and the banker was pleased at the hard bargaining he had done.

"I'll take your offer to them."

"I have a buyer in mind, but he won't be interested if you take too long."

Slocum hid his surprise. This was the first anyone had mentioned someone other than the banker being interested in the farm. He hesitated, then played a hole card to see what else might be in Goodman's deck.

"It might take a while to convince Marcus. As I said, he's plumb attached to that farm."

"There might be a fee in this for you, Slocum. Not too big, mind you, but something to recompense you for your trouble."

"I'll do my level best to have the papers signed by the end of the week. Is that good enough?" Slocum saw by the bright eyes and the slight smile curling Goodman's lips that it was. The tic twitched even harder, showing there was still stress involved, but the deal was eminently satisfactory. Slocum stood and thrust out his hand. Goodman shook with a surprisingly firm grip.

"It's a pleasure doing business with a man who knows how to get things done."

Slocum nodded to Goodman, then stepped out into the sultry day. Clouds dotted the distant horizon, promising rain later to cool off the stifling heat. But that was hours away. Turning toward the saloon, Slocum went to wet his whistle. He deserved a drop or two of liquid reward for the negotiations. He had read Goodman from the beginning and had even blundered into a better deal than he would have asked for. Laura and Cora would be happy to collect so much money.

Marcus Dahlquist was another matter. Slocum wondered if the young man wasn't losing his grip on his sanity and venturing into territory no one was comfortable in. If Marcus was going as crazy as a loon, then selling the farm was best so they could get him to a hospital where professionals could help him—or a sanitarium where he could be locked up so he wouldn't hurt himself or anyone else.

Slocum chanced a quick glance into the saloon before entering. Nobody in Bitter Creek had seen hide nor hair of Turner or his gang, but that didn't mean he shouldn't be cautious. Whatever Turner had in mind, he intended to use the town as his base. Without a marshal, he was the sole arbiter of the law—or lack of it.

"Hey, Slocum, come on in. A beer? Or you wantin' something stronger?" The barkeep hitched up his pants and reached for a beer mug.

"You read my mind," Slocum said. "There's nothing quite as quenching as a beer on a hot summer day."

"Not unless you have two of them. Get me one, too," said a voice down the bar from Slocum. Slocum reached for his six-shooter and then stopped before he drew. "Been a while since I laid eyes on you," Slocum said.

"More than two years, if I remember rightly, and I always do," said Joe Bench. He shoved out his calloused hand. Slocum shook, aware of how different Bench's hand was from the banker's. Goodman had a firm grip but a soft hand. There was nothing but calluses and muscle here.

"You must have gotten away from the posse," Slocum said, picking up his beer and going to a nearby table. The barkeep would eavesdrop the best he could, but Slocum preferred not to let him spy on them too easily. He and Joe Bench had not been on the right side of the law when they had ridden together in Texas. Still, without a marshal in town, what was the difference?

"They couldn't find their own asses with both hands, and I cleared out before they called in the Rangers," Bench said, laughing. He hefted a mug of beer and joined Slocum. Always alert, Bench sat so he could keep one eye on the door and his gun hand free to go for his six-shooter if the need arose.

Slocum guessed Bench was still on the run, if not from the law down Texas way, then possibly from Hanging Judge Parker's deputies out of Fort Smith. Enforcement in Indian Territory was spotty at best, but the judge's minions always returned with a suspect, even if he hadn't committed the crime they were trying to solve.

"I rode straight west until I got to the Rio Grande. I figured not even the Rangers would come after me since it was so easy to cross into Mexico," Slocum said. "Did you get away with the money from that stagecoach?"

"What's that? I thought you had it," Bench said. "Damnation, that driver took it! What a thief." Bench shook his head in dismay. "You can't trust nobody these days. He took the money, told the posse we'd stolen it, and probably lived high on the hog for a year or two."

"Not that long," Slocum said. "I've seen his kind. He spent it on booze and whores and gambled it away inside a month."

"Yeah, not like we wouldn't have done the same thing."

Slocum wondered if Bench was lying about taking the money. They hadn't planned the robbery too well and the federal marshal had sent out a posse to follow the stage. The robbery had just begun, Slocum and Bench with their guns leveled, when the posse had galloped into sight. Slocum had fled west and Bench had gone north. And the driver had stolen the money, blaming them for it. Maybe.

"Here's to successful escapes," Slocum said, lifting his mug. They clicked glasses and drank deeply. "What brings you to Bitter Creek?"

Bench looked hard at Slocum and said, "The same as you, I reckon."

Slocum considered how many beaus the Dahlquist sisters had and discarded the notion that Bench was among them. He was short, strong as a bull, and had an ugly face with a vicious scar across a mutilated left cheek, the product of a knife fight in Mesilla that had not gone well for him. Bench smelled like a goat, ate like a pig, and had the manners of a hungry coyote. There wasn't anyone Slocum would rather have watching his back, though. In spite of the outward appearances, Bench was as loyal as anyone Slocum had come across.

"I'm passing through," Slocum said.

"Looks like you've put down roots of some kind here," Bench said.

"What makes you say that?"

"I'd say you're waiting for him to show up. It was a mighty attractive offer and not one I'd pass on. You're the sort to deal yourself in, too."

"What's the game?"

"You don't know? This is rich." Bench finished off his beer, slammed it to the table, and bellowed for two more. After the barkeep delivered the beer, Bench went on. "I heard about him recruiting as I was making my way up along the Red River."

Slocum sipped at his beer, waiting for Bench to finish his story. After hearing about harrowing escapes from the Comanches and a Texas Ranger, he finally got to the part Slocum had already guessed.

"Yup, when I heard Monty Turner was recruiting and offering so much money, I knew I had to be part of it."

"Turner, eh?" Slocum worked on his beer. "He wants gunmen for his gang? What is he planning to do with this army he's recruiting?"

"He wants to control this section of Indian Territory. The law's nowhere to be seen. Hell, they don't even have a marshal in Bitter Creek. I asked. Turner intends to organize his gang to pick off every stage and shipment worth robbing. Doesn't want to let a single one get through. He has a special yen to rob every train rattling through, too."

"That's mighty efficient of him."

"He's a smart one, Slocum. So are you. You've come to join up, haven't you?"

"As I said, Bench, just passing through." Slocum finished the beer and stood. "Good seeing you again. And good luck finding Turner."

"I asked around town before I came in here. Finding him won't be a problem. You watch your back, Slocum."

"I always do."

Slocum stepped out into the heat and felt his clothing become plastered to his body by sweat that refused to evaporate. He walked down the street, got his horse, and started out of town, heading toward the Dahlquist farm. He had plenty to pass along.

As he rode, a dust cloud ahead obscured a rider, but whoever it was rode in the same direction. Slocum was in no particular hurry and considered what he wanted to do when he finally moved on. Laura was a creature of the big city, sophisticated and out of place on a farm. She would be even less likely to join him on the trail, wherever it led. He was more likely to join Monty Turner's gang than she was to come with him. He was still trying to figure how he thought about that when he reached the farmhouse. Laura came out as he dismounted.

"You took your time, John. What's happened?"

He wanted to talk it over with her before telling Marcus, but that wasn't going to be possible. Laura's brother came from the barn, looking chipper.

"You want to hear it at the same time as your brother?" he asked.

"Goodman agreed?"

Slocum nodded. Laura pursed her lips, then nodded, too, as Marcus stopped at the edge of the porch.

"Where you been, Slocum? There're chores needin' doin'."

"I spent some time talking with the banker." He outlined the deal Goodman had offered. He finished by saying, "Goodman has a buyer offering top dollar for the farm. I'd say take the deal. The money is decent, and you won't have to bring in the crops. That'll save a powerful lot of work and grief."

"Sell the farm? Sell it?" Marcus turned in a full circle, then threw up his arms and cried, "Why the hell not! We can make a profit off it. Thanks, Slocum, you've done some good work."

Slocum wondered if Marcus was trying to be sarcastic but he saw nothing but elation in the man's expression. But something didn't seem right. Marcus had wanted to hang on to his parent's legacy, no matter what the cost to him or his sisters.

Marcus danced up the steps and swept up Laura, whirled her about, and then dropped her back.

"I'll find Cora and let her know. You don't mind if I'm the one to tell her? Good." Marcus rushed into the farmhouse, leaving Slocum and Laura behind, staring at one another in wonder.

9

Slocum swung the ax high over his head and let gravity do some of the work splitting the firewood. The blade hit the wood with a satisfying *thunk!* He kicked away the pieces of split wood and put another log on the stump, trying to maintain a rhythm. Just as he began a new swing, he saw a cloud of dust building down the road leading to the farm. Whoever came rode fast and hard. He touched the bare spot on his left hip where his six-gun usually rode. He had left his pistol with his gear.

Hefting the ax, he started for the barn where he slept but hadn't gotten halfway there when he saw the solitary rider was only a youngster he had seen around Bitter Creek.

"Mr. Slocum, Mr. Slocum!" the boy called out, waving an arm around frantically. "There's been trouble aplenty in town."

Slocum abandoned his return to the barn for his gun and leaned on the ax handle, waiting for the breathless boy to tell about the trouble.

"He—he's dead. Shot in the back! Just like poor ole Hop Franks."

"Who do you mean?" Slocum asked.

"Th-they sent me from the bank. The head teller. He paid me a dime to come tell you. Mr. Goodman's been murdered, just like Hop Franks, and them outlaws done it! They gunned him down and robbed him and—"

"Whoa, slow down," Slocum said. "Take a deep breath, then give me the whole story."

It unwound slowly amid considerable speculation on the boy's part, but Slocum got the facts.

"Why'd anybody send you to tell me?"

"This place, the farm, you and him—Mr. Goodman—had a deal, and there won't be one now that he's dead. Nobody knows who owns the bank and people are all askin' fer their money back now and it's a lotta confusion. That's why."

"What's he mean, John?" Laura had come over to listen to the story. "The buyer doesn't want the farm anymore?"

"Goodman never said who he had hooked to buy the place," Slocum said. "I might find out who it was and make a deal directly. You'd get even more that way since Goodman wouldn't be taking a cut as agent." He also thought that if the bank goes out of business, the loan taken out by the elder Dahlquists could be ignored, giving Laura even more money.

"He's dead? Really and truly?" Marcus Dahlquist burst out laughing. "That's the way it goes, isn't it? Goodman's dead!" He went off humming a jaunty tune. Slocum frowned. Something wasn't right in the man's head. He had been as pleased as punch when it looked as if they'd sell the farm, and now he was equally happy that the banker had been murdered.

"Go on back to town and let the head teller know I'll be in right away. Is he running the bank?"

"Ain't nobody else who can. Mr. Goodman kept all his secrets . . . well . . . secret. Nobody knew anything about the bank or running it. Not really."

Slocum fished out a nickel and handed it to the grateful boy, who wheeled his lathered horse about and raced back to town.

"Does he mean it? That Goodman's business affairs went to the grave with him?" Laura frowned and looked as if she might burst into tears.

"Could be, but even the most secretive man has to leave notes or tell somebody what's going on. The teller must be keeping the bank open and might have seen or overheard Goodman talking to whoever's wanting to buy the farm." Slocum also considered the chance that the buyer would approach them directly, now that Goodman was dead.

"And you think you could find whoever it was Goodman had to buy the farm."

Slocum nodded. He looked past the woman to where her brother danced to music only he heard, using a fence post as a partner.

"Is Marcus right in the head?"

"He's been under so much strain since Papa and Mama died," Laura said, "that he has these spells. But they go away. When you find the buyer, I'm sure he'll be right as rain again."

"Go talk to him," Slocum said. "He was a mite too cheerful at the news of how Goodman died."

"You don't think he had anything to do with it, do you? Really, John. Marcus is my brother!" Laura headed for the impromptu square dance and joined Marcus.

Slocum went into the farmhouse and rummaged through the desk again. He took out the six-shooter and checked it once more. It hadn't been fired in some time and was still unloaded, as it had been the last time Slocum had looked at it. Even if Marcus had used it, then cleaned and oiled it, Slocum would have been able to tell. He shoved it back into the drawer and went to saddle his mare. He was getting tired of Bitter Creek and would clear out when he found the buyer for the farm. He owed Laura that much.

* * *

"We don't know what to do with the body," the head teller said, staring down at Goodman's corpse. "You got any ideas, Mr. Slocum?"

"Bury it."

"I mean, he was murdered and all. You can tell that. See? A single shot to the back of his head."

"There wasn't any reason to think Goodman would kill himself, was there?"

The question took the teller aback. His mouth opened, then snapped shut. He shook his head.

"There's not a whole lot to do about this since you don't have a marshal anymore," Slocum said. "There's no question how he died. What all was stolen?" Slocum looked around the bank. Goodman had been gunned down near his desk.

"Why, only what he had on him. I have no idea how much that would be, but Mr. Goodman was a frugal man. I never saw him carry more than a few dollars, mostly in small coins."

"He was a goddamn cheapskate," cut in another teller. The man stood with arms crossed and was scowling. "He never had more than five dollars on him. Said he might be tempted to give more to beggars, as if we had any in Bitter Creek. He always made sure the marshal got rid of any who drifted in."

"So his wallet was taken but nothing from the bank?"

"The vault wasn't even scratched," the head teller said. "Can't say whoever killed him didn't try to open the vault using the combination."

"Only Goodman had the combination," Slocum said. He had seen too many men like Goodman in his day. They trusted no one and hoarded their money. Whatever the combination was, he had committed it to memory and it wasn't written down anywhere.

"You're right, Mr. Slocum. He was the only one who knew it."

"Might be the robber tried to get him to open the vault, and he refused and got shot for his trouble," Slocum said. It was logical but didn't seem right, and he didn't know why.

"All it means is that we're out of jobs," complained the other teller. "Unless you blow open that vault, there's not going to be anyone to get into it this side of hell."

Slocum thought the teller was going to spit on the corpse but instead he turned and left, stripping off his cuff protectors and green visor as he went. With disdain, the teller tossed it all onto the floor and slammed the door as he left.

"There's going to be a powerful lot of trouble over this," the head teller said. He ran his hand through thinning hair. "I suppose I'm in charge, but there's nothing I can do."

"What's the trouble?"

"Everybody'll want their money out of the bank. That'll ruin the town."

"Let me see if I can't find something to help you out," Slocum lied. He stepped over Goodman's body and sat heavily in the banker's chair so he could riffle through the papers on his desk. He hunted for any hint as to who the buyer for the Dahlquist farm might be but found nothing. He leaned back and said, "Fetch the undertaker. Goodman is starting to smell up the lobby."

"I can't leave the bank," the teller started. Then he realized there was nothing to watch since nobody knew the combination to the vault. He bobbed his head and left Slocum behind.

Slocum went through a file cabinet, hunting for anything on the Dahlquist sale, but all he found were papers signed by Leon Dahlquist when he paid off the bank loan. Slocum tucked this into his pocket since it showed the farm was Marcus's. The Dahlquists obviously thought the banker was trying to foreclose but these papers showed the family owned the farm, free and clear.

To keep from pacing while he waited for the undertaker, he looked for any way to open the vault. He had robbed a bank or two in his day and knew how to use explosives to open even the toughest safe, but this one would result in most of the bank's interior being destroyed if adequate dynamite was used.

He looked up from his examination when the head teller and a man dressed in a black cloth cutaway frock coat entered. Slocum wondered if all undertakers had to have the same baleful look on their faces. This one had a long, hooked nose that added to the impression of being a vulture.

"The deceased," the undertaker said needlessly. He expertly went through Goodman's pockets and produced an expensive watch and gold jewelry from his cuffs and vest. Slocum watched in silence. If a robber had taken the watch and jewelry, he would have made more than the few dollars Goodman had in his wallet.

"The bullet killed him?" Slocum asked.

"A large caliber, fired in much the same fashion as the one that took poor Hop Franks's life," the man said in a deep, resonant voice, as if he practiced for the service.

"It has to be one of those owlhoots in the Turner Gang," said the teller. "They've got a reputation for shooting men in the back and then robbing them."

"I've heard that," Slocum allowed. "If the gang killed him, why didn't they blast open the vault?"

"I cannot say," said the undertaker. "No dynamite?"

"Seems mighty stupid of them to kill the only man who could open the vault and not have a way to get to the money."

"Criminals need not be geniuses," said the undertaker.

Slocum remembered what Joe Bench had told him of Turner's recruiting outlaws from all over the territory and how he intended to operate. Such planning didn't sound stupid at all and carried more than a good chance of succeeding.

Turner was a thinker as well as a killer. He wouldn't botch a bank robbery this badly, and even if he had, he would have been sure to notice the gold jewelry Goodman wore and steal it, too.

Slocum didn't like the feel of a murder where the killer made off with nothing more than five dollars.

"I don't think there'll be a run on the bank if you let everyone know you can't get to their money," Slocum told the teller.

"For two cents, I'd let somebody else deal with this," the man said, "but I've got my life savings in that vault. If I get it out, everyone else can have what's coming to them."

"I like the sound of that," Slocum said slowly. "Everyone should get what's coming to them."

He left the teller and undertaker bickering over how to pay for the funeral. He stepped up into his saddle and turned east, going back along the road he had ridden to get into Bitter Creek. As long as Monty Turner was in the region, he was going to be a thorn in Slocum's side. Not sure what he intended to do, Slocum rode for miles, hunting for any sign of the outlaw or his gang.

Just before sundown, he heard several gunshots, all coming in rapid succession. He trotted away from the road and circled, coming up a rise to a spot that overlooked the winding road farther along. Before the road twisted around and disappeared into a gentle valley, it crossed a stream. At this point three outlaws had ambushed a man driving a freight wagon.

Slocum could tell the driver had not been taken completely by surprise because he was crouched in the back of his wagon, firing a rifle at his attackers. One of his team lay dead, slumped in the harness and keeping the other horse from running away. The frightened survivor neighed and reared but was not strong enough or scared enough to drag the heavily laden wagon any distance. The constant tugging still made it difficult for the freighter in the rear to aim.

"Kill 'im, boys!" The command rang out and echoed down the valley. Slocum considered the distance to the fight and what he might do if he got there.

The driver answered all of Slocum's questions in a heartbeat. He stood, took aim, and fired. One road agent tumbled from the saddle even as the other two directed all their deadly fire in the man's direction. He jumped and jerked about before tumbling over the edge of the wagon bed. Even at this distance, Slocum saw that the man was dead.

"Why'd you do such a dumb thing as stand up?" Slocum wondered aloud. Then it came to him. The freighter had run out of ammo and wanted to make at least one shot count. He had swapped lives, his for an outlaw's. It was a desperate thing to do but Slocum approved. There was never any reason to die on your knees if you could go out with your gun blazing.

"Son of a bitch killed Jose," shouted the outlaw who had dismounted to tend his partner. "Shot him clean through the heart."

"Forget him. We got the whole damned wagon to ourselves. The boss is gonna like it."

"What was he carryin'?"

The first outlaw tore back the tarp and laughed.

"We hit the mother lode. He's got 'nuff food here to feed a town."

"Musta been freighting it over to Bitter Creek. They're sure gonna go hungry now."

"Let 'em starve. They didn't even replace the windows we shot up last time. Ain't as much fun shootin' at boards as it is knocking out big plate-glass windows."

The two outlaws started rooting through the supplies, sharing the choicer tidbits. Slocum slowly rode down the steep slope and found himself a gully to use to get even closer to the road agents as they enjoyed a feast on foodstuffs destined for Bitter Creek. He heard the two men laughing and tearing into airtights and offering samples of what they'd found to each other.

Slocum reached a spot where it would have been easy to shoot down both men, but he held back. He wanted to find Turner and his camp, not simply eradicate vermin like these. It took him a while to approach the wagon on foot, but the two owlhoots never heard or saw him in the twilight. They sat with their legs dangling at the back of the wagon. Several empty tins were scattered under their feet. They had gorged themselves on canned peaches and pears. Slocum knew they were close to being gorged when he heard one belch loud and long.

"Damn, that's good after all the crap we been eatin'. Turner ought to hire hisself a hunter who can bag more than a rabbit or two. I'm sick of fixin' my own food."

"You're lucky you ain't pizzened yourself," said the second outlaw.

Slocum crouched and hid when he saw both pairs of boots drop to the ground. The outlaws came around, easy targets if he had a mind to potshot them.

"What are we gonna do? One horse can't haul the wagon by itself."

"Cut the dead one loose and see if your horse won't pull in harness."

"My horse isn't broke for such work. Use yours."

"Might be we can get one horse to pull if we dump things from the load."

Slocum listened to the pair of them argue for ten minutes. Finally, the notion of leaving even a can of fruit or potted meat behind and having Turner find out settled the matter. One of the men hitched his horse into place. The surviving draft horse wasn't pleased with the newcomer beside him but both outlaws worked to quiet the equine fears and get the wagon rolling.

One road agent remained astride his horse while the other drove. As they rattled off into the night, Slocum went to the pile of empty tins and kicked at them. Then he saw to the driver and the fallen outlaw. The two had left their partner without any qualms. From what they had said, Jose was a newcomer to the gang. Slocum looked over the vaquero and decided he had only recently come up from Mexico, probably on the run from the law.

It was a chore he didn't much like, but it was a necessary one. He spent the next half hour burying both the driver and the outlaw in side-by-side graves. The soft ground let him dig easily enough, at least for a few feet. He should have planted them both deeper but didn't have the tools. If the coyotes wanted the bodies bad enough, digging them up wouldn't be difficult since all Slocum could do was place stones atop the graves.

He wiped off his hands, then mounted and followed the deep grooves cut into the soft earth by the stolen wagon. Even using only the bright starlight of the moonless night, he had no trouble trailing the two outlaws. Slocum took his time and made sure he wasn't riding into an ambush. Monty Turner had shown how adept he was at laying such traps.

An hour down the trail, Slocum heard the two outlaws arguing loudly. The rattle of the wagon convinced him they were still rolling along and must be getting near their camp. From what he could overhear, they each wanted to take credit for the food. Slocum smiled grimly. Some things never changed. During the war he had watched patrols return and argue over who had made the biggest kill, as if it mattered. Nobody was going to get a medal for such bloody work. Neither of the outlaws would get more than a passing nod of approval for bringing the food to the camp.

He slowed and eventually tugged back hard on the reins to stop his mare from advancing. The scent of dying fires reached his nose. Cocking his head to one side, he heard the wagon rattle to a halt and men shouting at the pair.

The camp was only a few dozen yards ahead.

Slocum started to dismount when he heard a sound that sent ice rippling through his veins. Behind him someone cocked a rifle. The hair on the back of his neck rose and he waited for the slug that would take his life because he had been too intent on the two wagon thieves and not careful enough looking out for the sentry he had known Turner would post.

It was almost a relief when he heard the command, "Move and you're a dead man."

10

"This must be the place," Slocum said. He kept his hands out away from his body to show he wasn't going for his six-shooter. Even if he tried, he could never outrun a bullet. He knew the rifle was centered on his back—and these men enjoyed gunning down their victims from behind.

"Whatcha goin' on about? What do you mean, this is the place? What kinda place you lookin' for?"

Slocum's mind raced. He had spoken only to gain himself some breathing room. If he didn't answer with something that satisfied the sentry, he was a dead man.

"He's here, isn't he?" Slocum looked over his shoulder but couldn't make out the outlaw too well. He stood in shadow and was dressed in dark-colored clothing. Even if Slocum had a definite target, he dared not draw and fire this close to Turner's camp. The whole gang would be on his neck in a split second.

"Who?"

"Bench," Slocum said. "Joe Bench. He was in Bitter Creek a while back, and asked if I wanted to join up."

"He one of the new guys?"

"There's nothing new about Bench. He's experienced. He's been around long enough to have a dozen 'Wanted' posters following him wherever he goes."

"A dozen? That all?" The guard snorted in contempt. "Hell, I got twice that. And the boss has even more."

"You mean Monty Turner? Bench said Turner was looking for some good men. I'm looking for a new outfit to ride with."

At this the guard decided not to kill Slocum.

"Let's me and you mosey on into camp. There might be a job for you, if you know this fellow Bench and if the boss likes your looks."

"Only the women like my looks," Slocum said, "and some of them complain if I give them the chance."

This provoked laughter from the guard, and Slocum knew he was in no immediate danger of getting cut down. He had to hope that Turner had never caught a good look at him. For once, Slocum was glad he had killed a man. Kent would have opened fire on him the instant he'd laid eyes on him.

"Keep the hands up where I kin see 'em," the sentry ordered. Slocum did as he was told as he marched forward toward the campfire. It was only his imagination but he felt as if he were on fire by the time he came within the circle illuminated by the bonfire the outlaws had built.

"What do you bring me, Jessup?" Monty Turner lifted himself on one elbow from where he sprawled back on his bedroll. Slocum couldn't miss that the outlaw's hand was hidden under a fold of blanket—and the distinctive outline of a six-gun was apparent in the dancing firelight.

"This owlhoot said he knows Joe Bench and wants to join us."

"Bench? I don't know any Bench," Turner said.

Slocum sucked in his breath and considered his chances. They were terrible. A half dozen outlaws gathered by the fire, all with their hands resting on the butts of their six-guns. Even if he could get off a shot or two, the rifle pointed at his spine insured nothing but a quick death unless he bluffed his way through.

"The hell you don't," Slocum said, his eyes coming to rest on a short, shadowy figure striding purposefully toward the fire. "That's Joe Bench. Or did you give them a summer name, Joe?"

"Slocum, I didn't think you were interested in joining up."

"You know him?"

"John Slocum," Bench said. "Me and him, we been partners off and on for a couple years. Not so much lately since we rode different trails."

"He's not likely to be wearing a badge?" Turner twisted enough to point his six-shooter at Slocum. The thin blanket wouldn't do much to deflect the bullet if he fired.

"Only if he cut down a marshal and wanted to show off a trophy," Bench said, laughing. "I'd trust him with my life."

"Then that's what you're gonna do," Turner said.

"What do you mean?" Bench turned cold and squared off, his hand near the iron on his hip.

"You vouch for him. If he turns out to be the law, you both die."

Bench relaxed and laughed again.

"Ain't no chance of that. Him bein' the law, I mean. Reckon we're both gonna die sooner or later. With Slocum at my back, it's likely to be later. I trust him, and you can, too."

Slocum saw Monty Turner take his hand off the hidden pistol so he could lounge back, his fingers laced and tucked under the back of his head so he could stare up into the night sky.

"Looks like a summer gully washer is on the way," Turner said. "You better get bedded down, Slocum. Show him what's what, Bench."

"Come on, John. I pitched my camp yonder. The fire's enough to keep the pair of us warm tonight."

Slocum's shoulders almost knotted from strain. He ambled after Bench but felt the eyes on him. As he walked, he imagined all the road agents drawing and firing squarely into his back.

He and Bench fetched his horse. Slocum noticed that the guard he had encountered at first still trailed them, fingering the trigger of his rifle as if he was itching to cut them both down. He probably was.

"Not a friendly bunch," Slocum said as he spread his bedroll out under a tree. In spite of what Turner had said, it didn't look like a storm brewing to Slocum—not that kind of storm, at least.

"They'll get to know you. Don't mention that you rode with Quantrill, though. Some of these here boys hail from Kansas and probably were Jayhawkers. Mostly they don't care, but some can get a mite touchy about the war and all."

"They won. What's to get a nervous trigger finger over?"

"They mighta fought for the Federals but they got Union cavalry on their asses all the time. There's no love lost between them and the boys in blue."

"Good to know," Slocum said, sprawling back and wondering what the hell he had blundered into. If the fires died and the sentries grew sleepy, he would sneak away. That would put Bench in a dangerous spot, but he had to know when he joined up how likely he was to get shot in the back by this bunch.

"We got a big robbery planned for the morning," Bench said, obviously anxious to impress Slocum. "There's a gold shipment on its way to Fort Gibson. Payroll."

"The army pays its soldiers in paper money," Slocum said.

"Not this time. There've been deserters aplenty and this is their way to hangin' on to a few of the veterans."

"Might be a trap," Slocum said.

"Turner's got it all planned out," Bench said. "He's got somebody on the inside feedin' him all he needs to know."

"Has this gang done any robberies together before?"

"I suppose so," Bench said, scratching his head. "What's that got to do with the job tomorrow?"

Slocum said nothing. This might be Turner's way to see who was loyal and who wasn't. If the army planned a trap—and Slocum smelled something rotten about the robbery from a mile off—Turner might be willing to lose a few recruits to see how they all fought and if any of them looked as if he knew it was a trap by hanging back. They might either be a coward, in which case he didn't want them riding with him, or they could be a federal deputy and more than worthy of a bullet for their treachery.

"You worry about the damnedest things, Slocum. Makes a body wonder about you at times."

Slocum lay and listened to the road agents slowly going to sleep all around. What worried him the most was the steady movement in the underbrush all around him. Turner must have alerted the guards to watch for any attempt to bolt for freedom. They watched him, and never once did he have the feeling they would get tired of patrolling, sit for a spell, then drift off to sleep thinking they were doing their jobs. Turner had put the fear into them—or maybe they simply disliked Slocum.

He hadn't seen any of the men who might recognize him. But resting easy still eluded him. In spite of his worry, Slocum rolled onto his side and eventually drifted to sleep. He awoke with a start, hand wrapped around his six-shooter, when Bench shook his shoulder.

"Rise and shine. We got to be on the road to lay the ambush 'fore the cavalry knows what's happening."

The others in the camp grumbled and moaned about rising before the sun, but Slocum took a cup of boiled coffee and let it trickle down his throat. It had the kick of a mule and his alertness was soon guaranteed by the way the coffee puddled in his belly and spread warmth throughout his body.

"Mount up, boys," Turner called. "You know where to go and what to do. Don't change anything from the plan I gave you."

"What are you supposed to do?" Slocum asked Bench.

"Let you tag along, I reckon," Bench said. "Don't worry. There'll be enough gold to go around. You'll get your share."

Turner eyed him and Bench but said nothing. The outlaw leader trotted off into the sunrise, but Bench steered them in another direction.

"We got a spot on the road to watch. Nobody gets past us, no matter what direction they're comin' from."

"How are two guns supposed to stop a company of soldiers?"

"Not a company. Turner said there ain't more than ten or so troopers on patrol right now. None of them's gonna be guardin' the gold shipment." Seeing Slocum's skepticism, Bench went on to explain. "See? They been hit too many times before, so this time they're tryin' to sneak the gold past us. No guards other than the shotgun guard with the driver."

None of this made sense to Slocum, but he rode with Bench until the other man finally fell silent after having explained all he could. Slocum had the feeling that after relaying the plan, Bench was feeling a mite uneasy himself. It might have sounded all right when Turner sketched it out, but explaining it revealed the problems—and the obvious dangers.

"This is the spot," Bench said, sliding his rifle from its scabbard. "You want to take the other side of the road?"

Slocum studied the possible spots where he might hide and finally shook his head.

"Nothing across the road. We don't need to keep them in a cross fire when they come, either. I get in the rocks above you and we can both cover more of the road. If I'm over there, about the only one I could shoot would be you."

"You thinkin' that's what Turner had in mind?" Bench asked.

"You said it. Not me." Slocum secured his and Bench's horses, then climbed up the loose rock on the hillside above the road to a spot where he commanded a stretch almost a hundred yards wide. If Turner had chosen this ambush, he had done a good job. Slocum couldn't have picked a better spot himself.

"See anything, John?"

"I'll go higher," he answered. Making his way up the steep slope as sure as any mountain goat, he reached the ridge and squinted into the rising sun. Using his hand to shield his eyes, he peered at the road. His breath came a little faster when he saw the dust cloud moving slowly in their direction.

"I see it, too, John. We got ourselves a robbery!" Bench cocked his rifle and trained his sights on the road, should the driver succeed in getting away from the rest of the road agents.

Slocum watched but didn't see Turner and the others swooping down on the wagon.

"The other direction!" Slocum called. "We've got company coming from the other side!"

He swung about and sighted down his rifle barrel at a pair of riders walking along the road in their direction. Slocum lowered the rifle to get a better look at the two men. Neither was aware of the robbery going on a half mile in front of them along the road, and each rode as if he hadn't a care in the world. They might have been heading to a Sunday social for all the awareness they showed.

"Them deputies?" Bench rose from his secure spot lower on the hill and worked to find a new line of fire.

"Don't shoot," Slocum said. "They aren't a threat."

Barely had the words come from his lips before one of the riders spotted him and pointed. Both men stopped and stared up the hill. Either Bench saw something Slocum didn't, or he merely panicked and fired. His round missed both men by a country mile, but it spooked their horses and made an accurate shot at this range impossible.

"Hold your fire, Bench," Slocum shouted. "We don't want them getting away to bring the law down on us."

"Then we gotta kill the both of 'em!" Bench stood and began firing with more methodical intent now. He had calmed, and Slocum knew he was a deadly accurate shot.

One rider slumped in the saddle, grabbing his belly. One shot from Bench's rifle had found its target. The other man yanked out his rifle and began firing wildly. What he lacked in accuracy he made up for in luck. A bullet whined off the rock in front of Bench and knocked him backward.

"You hurt? Bench? Bench!" Slocum didn't try to bring down the man firing at them. He slipped and slid down the slope until he reached his partner. Bench was pale but cussing a blue streak.

"Slug ripped through my side," he grated out. "Hurts like hellfire." Bench laughed ruefully and said, "Hurts worse'n the time me and you tried that chili pepper from Mexico. I swear I thought I'd swallowed a wasp what stung my mouth and swallow pipe."

"You're all right," Slocum said. In spite of the blood soaking Bench's shirt, the wound was minor. The ricochet had cut through Bench's gun belt and tore a hunk of flesh away in a ragged gash. It looked worse than it was, and his friend was probably right: It hurt like a son of a bitch but wasn't going to kill him.

"You offered me a quart of beer down in Mexico," Bench said. "Made me feel just fine, in spite of the pepper burnin' my guts out."

"I don't have any beer to give you now, and if I did, I'd drink it myself," Slocum said. He lifted his head just above the rock. He retreated twice as fast when another bullet ripped through the crown of his hat and sent it flying.

"He's a damned sight better marksman than he has any

right to be," Bench said, struggling to sit up. He winced, pressed his left hand to his side, and chanced a quick look around the edge of the rock. "Don't look like the law."

"Just some pilgrim riding along, minding his own business and getting shot at," Slocum said. Calling out to the men below on the road wasn't likely to have much effect. "I don't want to shoot him unless I have to. He didn't start this dustup."

"Me wingin' his friend means he's got blood in his eye. I did just *wing* him, didn't I? If I killed him, his partner might never go away without being filled with lead, too."

Slocum retrieved his hat, pushed it up to draw fire while he peeked around the side of the rock. This time the rifleman was too cagey to be lured into shooting and wasting his ammo. He sat astride his horse, keeping careful aim and waiting for a substantial target before firing again.

"Turner wanted us to keep the lawmen away from the ambush site," Slocum said. "These might not be deputies, but we're keeping them away anyway."

"Fat lot of good that does me. I'm still bleedin' like a son of a bitch!"

Slocum heard the annoyance in Bench's tone, not real pain. He ignored the complaint and began working his way back up to where he had first spotted the riders. From there he had a clear field of fire. The men—especially the one doing the shooting—weren't fools. Once they saw he held the high ground, they would hightail it back the way they came. If for no other reason than that the one needed a doctor to pull Bench's slug from his belly.

Two rounds whined off rocks near Slocum, but he kept moving. Hitting him at this distance while mounted proved too difficult for the rifleman. Slocum regained his perch and took a quick look along the road. The wagon driver had not been waylaid yet and drove closer by the minute. Slocum wasn't sure why Turner hadn't attacked. The position farther back along the road was perfect for an ambush, but he couldn't let the wagon rattle on below where he and Bench were positioned. The two riders would find two more allies. The driver, the guard, and the two riders would outgun them.

Slocum started to take a shot at the wagon, then was driven down by furious fire from the other direction. He settled down, rested his rifle on the top of a rock, and waited for the shot. During the war he had been one of the CSA's top snipers. That had required both patience and marksmanship. All he had to do now was get off one good shot.

He squeezed the trigger, felt the rifle recoil into his shoulder, and knew he had not allowed for the elevation. His slug hit the rifleman's horse and brought it to its knees.

"Damn, Slocum, why are you killin' horses? You hungry enough to eat the meat?"

Slocum tried to ignore Bench's taunt. He adjusted his gunsight, but the rider had dropped off the felled horse and took refuge behind its dead body. Unless he had a mountain howitzer, he was never going to hit the cowering man now. He looked back toward the wagon and saw Turner had finally sprung the trap. A half dozen road agents closed in on the wagon. The guard threw up his hands in surrender. Slocum saw one of the outlaws shoot him in the back. Then he found himself occupied with staying alive again.

The man hiding behind the dead horse had bolted for his partner, who was slumped over but still in the saddle. The wounded man reached down and caught his friend's arm, lifting him into the saddle behind him. The horse staggered under the double weight but wheeled about. As they galloped away, the second rider fired until his rifle came up empty. Even at this distance, Slocum heard the metallic click as the hammer fell on an empty chamber.

"You ran 'em off, John," gloated Bench. "And lookee there. Turner's finally decided to make us all rich."

Slocum stood to get a better look at the robbery in progress. For a moment he couldn't figure out what was wrong.

Then he realized that the driver lay sprawled in the wagon bed, joining his guard in death. But the tarp was only untied at the rear and huge lumps showed cargo remained un- touched—unlooted.

Of Turner and the others Slocum saw nothing. Then an explosion shook the ground and lifted Slocum off his feet. He spun through the air and landed hard enough to be stunned. Gasping for breath, he tried to sit up. Then the dawn sky turned black again as he passed out.

11

The world shook all around him. In the distance he heard a ringing sound and his name being called. The name came faint and distant and—

He snapped awake, struggling to grab his six-shooter. A strong hand clamped on his wrist and prevented him from drawing.

"You settle down now, you hear?" Bench had to hang on to him as he fought.

"Not hearing too good," Slocum said. He realized he was shouting but could hardly hear himself. Jerking free of Bench's bloody grip, he sat up and shook his head to see if anything had rattled loose. He was sorry he made the attempt. Sharp pain lanced down hard behind his eyes and made him sick to his stomach.

"The explosion," Bench grated out. "It was the explosion that did that to you."

"What blew up?" Slocum regained some of his wits, forced himself to his feet, and looked down toward the road. The sun had risen fully above the horizon, warning him that he had been unconscious for several minutes. A world of trouble could fall on him in that time.

He looked around for any sign of Turner and the rest of the gang, but they were nowhere to be found. Where the wagon had come to a halt, where he had seen the driver and guard both sprawled in the bed, was nothing more than a deep crater. Smoke rose from the sides and, if he let his imagination run wild, pieces of the wagon lay scattered about, both in the crater and along the roadside.

"It blew up." He felt both numb and a little dumb making the statement.

"Went up like a Fourth of July skyrocket," Bench said. "You got any ideas why that happened, John?"

"Dynamite. There must have been a couple dozen cases of dynamite in that wagon. They all blew at the same time. Had to, to make a hole that deep."

"Accident?"

Slocum doubted that. Dynamite was hard to set off without a blasting cap. It could be frozen and fried and even tossed around, if you were careful enough. It took the sharp explosion of a blasting cap to detonate. Whatever had happened in the wagon was not an accident.

"Might be the driver done it. He saw he was bein' robbed and—"

"The driver was dead," Slocum said, cutting Bench off. "He was flopped in the rear of the wagon and couldn't have set it off."

"Might have been smokin' a cigar. That coulda set it off," Bench said reluctantly. Even he did not believe that had happened.

Slocum made his way down the far side of the hill to stand on the edge of the crater. The distinctive odor of detonated dynamite filled his nostrils. His stomach heaved a mite when he saw a burned, severed arm on the far side of the crater. He had walked through battlefields and seen bits and pieces of mutilated soldiers but that had been a long time back. He thought he had put such things behind him.

He obviously had not.

"Where'd Turner and the gang go?" Bench looked around rather than into the crater. Slocum turned away. He had seen enough, too.

"There," he said, pointing to a cloud of dust settling on the prairie. Conflicting emotions raged inside him. He wanted to know what was going on, but common sense told him to get on his mare and get the hell back to Bitter Creek. He could warn the Dahlquists that Turner and his gang were becoming bolder—but Laura and Cora already knew that. Slocum wasn't sure their brother would much care. Marcus had turned downright loony.

He ought to step up into the saddle and ride south, away from everything, but curiosity took its toll on sound judgment.

"Get the horses," Slocum ordered. "You're up for that, aren't you?" He didn't bother looking at Bench. He knew the outlaw was only slightly inconvenienced by the wound along his left hip bone. Keeping Turner and his gang in sight mattered more to keep them from returning and—

And what? Slocum was damned if he knew what was going on, but he intended to find out.

"You think they thought we was dead, John?"

Slocum mounted and looked at his friend. Bench was nobody's fool, but he seemed honest with the question.

"It didn't matter to Turner," Slocum said.

"They intended to cut us out of the gold," Bench said, his mouth becoming a thin line. His gun hand flexed. If Monty Turner had been anywhere in sight, Bench would have shot him. This made Slocum consider what he really wanted to do. If they overtook Turner and his gang, there would be gunplay unless things were put straight in Bench's mind. Slocum had seen the wagon guard shot from behind. For all he knew, the driver had been, too.

"Let's find out," Slocum said, putting his heels to his mare's flanks. He aimed straight for the dust cloud, but it died down as they rode. Slocum continued on instinct rather than any tracking ability. The prairie had been cut up from a herd of cattle grazing here, but he figured Turner had no reason to lay a false trail. If he had headed north, he would keep riding north.

And he had. Slocum and Bench overtook the gang within the hour.

Jessup, the guard from the night before, spotted them almost immediately as they rode down into a ravine where the gang had stopped.

"Hey, boss. We got company!" Jessup bellowed. He hefted his rifle but did not point it in Slocum's direction. If he had he would have died on the spot. The more he had ridden the outlaws' trail, the angrier Slocum had become.

The others looked up but were unconcerned. Turner hitched up his gun belt and came over to talk. Slocum looked for any hint of treachery. If Turner's eyes flickered so much as a little to someone behind intending to shoot them in the back, Slocum would throw down on him and get at least two rounds off before anyone could kill him.

"Wondered where the pair of you got off to," Turner said.

"We want our cut. You're not tryin' to do us out of what's rightfully ours, are you?" Bench glowered. Turner glanced at him, disregarded the man's anger, and spoke straight to Slocum.

"You have the look of bein' in a fight."

"Two riders," Slocum said. "We took care of them." He didn't bother explaining he had only run them off. If they complained to a federal marshal or the cavalry, all Indian Territory would be on the lookout for Turner and his road agents.

"Figured you could, if anyone was able to come through for me," Turner said, nodding slowly. He pursed his lips, studied them, and finally said, "You goin' to sit on them

horses all day or you want some coffee? Got a pot brewin'
while I explain the robbery."

"Nothing to explain," Slocum said. "The damned wagon
blew up."

Turner laughed harshly. "Not *that* robbery. I only needed
a couple cases of dynamite, so we blew up what we couldn't
haul off."

"There wasn't any gold?" Bench looked ready to boil
over. "We risked our damn fool necks and there was never
any gold?"

"I didn't say that," Turner snapped. "We had to get the
dynamite to get to the gold. You weren't dumb enough to
believe the army'd move the gold on a wagon with only a
single guard, were you? They're transportin' it by train."

"You're going to blow up the railroad tracks to stop the
train?" asked Slocum.

"I'm goin' to blow up the tracks *under* the train. I want
it derailed to give everybody somethin' more to worry over.
The railroad company has to repair tracks and put their cars
back on the line. Passengers will complain. People will
send off angry telegrams to who the hell knows who, de-
mandin' action. And we'll waltz away with enough gold for
each and every one of us to live on for a year."

Slocum remembered what he had heard. Turner wanted
to pluck clean the entire territory, not letting a single shipment of value slip through his hands. More than this,
Slocum remembered somebody saying that Turner had a
grudge against the railroad. He was spinning a tall tale
again to gull Bench into playing along one more time.
What his game was, Slocum couldn't tell, but it might be
an army gold shipment. Eventually, Turner had to pay off
his men or they would drift away—or worse. None of
them looked like the sort to take kindly to not having specie riding in their saddlebags when they'd been promised
some.

"When?" Slocum asked.

"Yeah, when we gonna be rollin' in the gold?" asked Bench.

"You two got ants in your pants? Climb down, have that coffee. Jessup's got a pint of whiskey he'll share. Won't you, Jessup?" Turner glanced over his shoulder to where his guard looked pissed at having his private stock given away without his permission.

"Yeah, right, boss. Whatever you say."

"You'll be able to buy a case of Billy Taylor's finest Kentucky whiskey with your share of the gold," Turner said. "Right now, you'll be buyin' a share of friendship with our two new friends." With that Turner spun and walked back to the fire. An outlaw handed him a tin cup brimming with coffee.

Slocum dismounted and said to Jessup, "I'll just have the coffee."

As the man began to grin at keeping his whiskey for his own thirst, Bench piped up, "I'll take a nip or two, if you got the bottle handy."

Jessup pulled the bottle from his hip pocket and passed it to Bench, who proceeded to knock back enough of the tarantula juice to get knee-walking drunk. Slocum ignored the two and went to look at the crude map Turner had scratched into the bottom of the muddy ravine.

"We're here, maybe a mile from the tracks," Turner explained, pressing the toe of his boot into the mud. "Over here is where we plant the charges along the tracks. I want at least fifty feet of track blown to hell and gone."

"Why so much?" Slocum asked.

"I can't be sure of the timing, so when we see the train chuggin' our way, you light the fuse and run like hell, Slocum. Timing doesn't have to be exact as long as some of the track is under part of the train."

"Is it a long train? Or a passenger train?" Slocum asked. Seeing Turner's expression, he explained. "Passenger trains aren't as long. Maybe ten cars. A freight train could be thirty."

"I see," Turner said. "You boys listen up to what Slocum is sayin'. He's thinkin' this through. It's a passenger train with a mail car." Turner looked hard at Slocum and said, "That suit you?"

"Just fine."

"Glad to hear it. Now, here's how I want you deployed."

Slocum watched as Turner set up the attack. He grudgingly approved of the plan when Turner pointedly asked for his opinion. Turner was as good as any general Slocum had seen at planning his tactics.

"Mount up and we ride," Turner said, glancing at the sun halfway up the sky. "We don't have much time, since the train comes through in an hour. Maybe less."

Slocum mounted and saw that Bench had some trouble staying in the saddle.

"Too much booze?" he asked.

"Never be too much whiskey," Bench said, then belched and wobbled around like a child's spinning top about to come to rest. He righted himself and stared ahead. "You think this plan's good, Slocum?"

"I do." A dozen different schemes flashed through Slocum's head. He might end up with enough gold to forget Laura and her family problems and find himself a place to hole up. If Turner was right, stealing this much gold would bring down the wrath of the entire government on their heads. Even if Turner wasn't telling the truth about how much the army payroll was, the railroad would send Pinkertons out to put an end to such robberies. Destroying track and frightening passengers was not something the train owners could tolerate for long.

Or even for one time. If someone robbed their railroad once, he would be emboldened and do it again. And again.

"There it is," Turner called. "Get that dynamite laid out. You want to tell 'em where to plant it, Slocum?"

"Why do you think I know anything about explosives?"

Slocum had worked as a blaster on and off in hard-rock mines and could get twice the result any of Turner's men likely could, but he wasn't about to admit his experience. The less Turner knew about him, the better. He had seen how cunning the outlaw could be.

"I figured you were goin' to light the fuse so you might want a say-so about where the dynamite's placed."

"Fair enough." Slocum looked at Bench and worried about the man's ability to think fast, should the need arise.

When the need arose.

"You ever handle dynamite before?" Slocum asked of Jessup when he saw how gingerly the man carried a case. He acted as if the slightest jolt would set it off.

"Sure, plenty of times," the man lied.

Slocum rode up and down the tracks, hunting for the right spot, but it hardly mattered where they planted the explosives. The tracks ran off in both directions until they collapsed to shiny pinpoints on either horizon. This part of Indian Territory was more prairie than hill country.

"Plant a stick on every railroad tie," Slocum ordered. "Be sure each stick is pressed hard against the steel rail. String some fuse from every other stick and tie it all into a single fuse." He had to show Jessup what he meant but when he finished, he had a spiderweb of fuse laid out on either side of the tracks.

"When I give the word, you light the single fuse on the other side," Slocum said.

"And it'll burn down to the knot and set off each of the other fuses, all of them runnin' to a stick of dynamite. Pretty clever, Slocum." Jessup frowned. "How come we didn't run fuse to all the sticks?"

"When some go off, the shock along the rails ought to be enough to set off the rest."

He pulled out his pocket watch and checked it. A quarter till noon. Slocum tucked it back, wondering when the train was due. He stood on the track and felt a tiny quiver.

"Train's coming," he said. "Get yourself a smoke before we go to light the fuse."

Jessup fumbled to roll a cigarette. He was so nervous he spilled most of the fixings. Slocum worked on one of his own more deliberately. He knew they had plenty of time before the train came.

"Light the damn fuse!" Turner shouted from fifty yards away. "The train's in sight!"

Slocum had about finished his cigarette. He saw Jessup clumsily press the hot coal of his smoke to the fuse. It sizzled, popped, and began to burn. Seconds later, Slocum had his fuse lit, too. He ran like the demons of hell were on his tail because he knew the damage so much dynamite could do. Even if he had misjudged the time, enough track would be blown up to make it dangerous to be anywhere nearby.

He skidded around in the soft earth and dropped into a shallow gully beside Bench. The man looked more sober now, the thrill of the robbery burning away the alcoholic fog.

"We're gonna do it, Slocum. We gonna get rich today. I can feel it in my bones."

Less than a minute later, Slocum felt something else in his bones. The train came rumbling up and past and then the dynamite detonated. Before, back on the hill, he had been caught unaware. Not now. The ground shook and metal screeched as track disappeared in front of the speeding train. The engine kept rolling without the benefit of rails for a few yards and then slewed to one side. The couplings on the back four cars separated, letting them roll to a halt. The first passenger car hit the breach in the steel rail, then tipped to the side and crashed to the ground amid a cloud of dust and torn-up prairie weeds. The remainder of the cars stayed upright on the tracks behind.

"Let's get rich, men!" Turner ran forward, waving his six-shooter in the air.

Slocum followed, not wanting to turn his back on the outlaw or any of those in his gang.

12

Slocum held back just a little to see what the others did. Bench let out a rebel yell and ran beside Jessup toward the freight car that had fallen to its side, snapping the coupling from the caboose behind and the passenger car in front of it. Turner obviously intended to play on the confusion to rob the passengers. Slocum joined Bench and Jessup in trying to force open the freight car door.

"Damn thing's jammed up," Bench complained. He stepped back and wiped sweat off his forehead. "Who woulda thought robbin' a train would be this much work?"

Slocum jumped onto the side of the car and went to a gaping hole. When the freight car had hit the ground, it had twisted around, tearing wood and steel as easily as if they had been paper. Cautiously peering inside, he saw a mail clerk sprawled gracelessly across a huge safe that had come loose from its moorings.

"I only see one man inside, and he isn't in any condition to put up a fight," Slocum called. About this time, Jessup and Bench pried open the door enough to let in a shaft of sunlight.

"Look out!" Slocum shouted. There had been another man inside, a well-armed guard who opened fire with a scattergun. The blast filled the freight car and rolled across the prairie. Almost instantly came return fire from both Bench and Jessup. Slocum wasn't sure which one cut down the guard. It didn't matter since the aim was deadly.

Slocum tore at the hole until it was big enough for him to drop down through. He landed on the sloping floor and grabbed on to the safe. It shifted and caused the dead mail clerk to flop off the top.

"We need to blow it," Slocum said. "Unless Turner has the combination."

"I put away a few sticks just for this, Slocum," came Turner's amused voice. "You know enough to blow the safe?"

"I'm out of practice," Slocum said. Both Bench and Jessup rummaged through the stack of mail bags. Sometimes people send cash in thick packets. That was chicken feed compared to what Turner promised was inside the safe. Slocum stared down Turner, who finally broke off and bellowed to others outside to fetch the explosive.

"You finish robbing the passengers?" Slocum asked.

"They were a poverty-stricken lot," Turner said. He looked hard at Slocum. "You sound like you don't approve of takin' every nickel we can find. You against such thievin'?"

"I want what's in here," Slocum said, patting the iron safe. "If you have it right, there's gold inside."

"What's that supposed to mean?" Turner squared off. Slocum was at a disadvantage, propped against the safe on the sloping floor while Turner balanced in the open doorway.

"If the army was moving a shipment, why isn't there a soldier guarding the car? Or several?"

"I told you. They wanted to do this on the sly. Now quit your bellyachin' and get out of the way, unless you want me to cram the dynamite up your ass before I light it."

Slocum took the chance to crawl crablike along the

floor until he could pull himself up and out. Turner and another member of the gang set the dynamite. Slocum saw that they were experts at such blasting and he could not have planted the charge better himself. When it cut loose, it would create the most damage to the safe while doing as little as possible to the safe's contents.

"Fire in the hole!" Turner vaulted from the car and ran a few paces. Slocum followed more slowly. He had seen Turner cut a foot of waxy black miner's fuse and knew he had a full minute to get clear.

He knelt down, facing away, and clapped his hands over his ears just as the dynamite detonated. The ground shook but not like it had when he had derailed the train. Debris showered down as Turner and the others rushed back to see what they had exposed in the safe.

"We done it, Slocum, we done it!" whooped Bench. "The whole damned safe's crammed with sacks of gold coins! There must be a thousand dollars inside!"

Turner grunted, heaved, and passed the first of the sacks of coins to his henchmen. They formed a bucket brigade and moved six of the heavy sacks from the train. By this time two others in the gang had brought up their horses. Slocum noticed for the first time they had three spares to carry the gold. Again he had to admit grudging admiration for the way Monty Turner had organized the raid. He obviously had expected to find the gold since he had brought along an adequate number of horses to get it away from the scene of the crime.

"Load up the packhorses," Turner called as he scrambled from the freight car. "The rest of you, go make sure we're not leavin' any witnesses." He stared straight at Slocum. "What're you waitin' for? You too good to take my orders?"

"There's no need to kill the passengers and crew," Slocum said.

"When you're leadin' this here gang, you can give the orders. Now do it or join them." Turner jerked his thumb over his shoulder to indicate the pair of dead men inside the freight car.

Slocum felt eyes on him and knew more than one six-shooter had been leveled. It wouldn't take much for lead to start flying. The more in the gang who died, the bigger the cut for those remaining after the bloodshed. Slocum wondered if Turner hadn't intended for more to die in the robbery and was disappointed everything had gone so smoothly.

"I'll come with you, John," Bench said. He drew his six-gun and stalked alongside until they were out of earshot of Turner and the rest of the gang. "There's no call for wanton killin'," Bench said. "Who's gonna even notice the gold's gone? The railroad will worry more about repairin' the track and gettin' cars upright than something sent by the damned army."

"I don't think it was any cavalry payroll," Slocum said. "I don't know where it was bound, but it wasn't guarded right for the army to have anything to do with it."

"That was real strange they didn't have a squad of soldiers inside," Bench allowed. "What else do those blue-bellies have to do other than sit around their camps and get fat? Who do you suppose the money belongs to?"

"Somebody likely to get real mean about recovering it," Slocum said. "If I can get a look at the bags holding the coins, that might give us something to chew on awhile."

"I saw the sacks," Bench said, "but me and book learnin', well, we're pretty much strangers. I can write my own name, though."

"Might not matter whether it's Pinkertons or cavalry on our trail," Slocum said. He poked his head into the first passenger car. A half dozen injured men moaned and feebly tried to get out from under seats and one another. They lay in a pile against a section of seats.

"What are we gonna do? I don't cotton much to mur-derin' 'em in cold blood. I ain't a milksop, but there's no point in wastin' good ammo on men who don't deserve to die, other than they had the misfortune to be on the wrong train," Bench said.

Slocum nodded in approval. He and Bench had gotten along well because they shared a similar enough view of the world not to get on each other's nerves. Both of them had seen too much savage, senseless killing to indulge themselves in more.

"Don't go reaching for a pistol," Slocum warned one man. He didn't heed Slocum, drew, and fired. The slug ripped through the wood above Slocum's head. A second round came closer. Ducking and weaving, Slocum drew his fire until his six-shooter came up empty. "Don't reload," Slocum ordered. He sighted down the barrel of his Colt so the man stared into the bore. The man, a peddler, given the cut of his clothing, closed his eyes and resigned himself to dying.

Slocum backed away and went to the next car. The passengers here were all dead or unconscious. He moved to the front passenger car where Bench clubbed a man who tried to stick a knife into his gut.

"Feisty little bantam rooster of a fella," Bench said with some admiration. "Not up to the chore of killin' me."

"Let's go," Slocum said. He fired his pistol until it came up empty, then reloaded as he walked back to the horses. It didn't surprise him much that Turner and the rest had already left. What did surprise him was that Turner had left his and Bench's horses behind, almost as if they were actually part of the gang and knew to catch up.

"We better hurry 'fore them bastards spend our cut of the loot," Bench said, stepping up into the saddle.

Slocum considered his options. This would be a good time to simply ride back to Bitter Creek—or anywhere else. Turner wouldn't complain because there'd be a bigger slice of the pie for everyone in the gang, but Slocum had questions he wanted answered. The only person who could give him those answers rode along with the gold.

"Let's watch our backs real close," Slocum said as he mounted and trotted alongside Bench.

"Always, John. You know me. Careful's my middle name. That and Adam. Joseph 'Damned Careful' Adam Bench, that's me!" Bench laughed at his own joke while Slocum fell into deep thought as he rode, following the easy trail cut in the soft prairie.

A new thunderstorm brewed on the horizon ahead.

Burdened by the gold, the road agents couldn't make as good a time as Slocum and Bench. Within the hour, they overtook Turner in spite of the outlaw's many turnings and twistings, trying to confuse the trail.

"Hey, boss, they finally showed up!" Jessup called. The outlaw lowered his rifle and waved to them as they rode up. Turner had camped in a ravine that would fill with sudden water if the storm moved much closer, but Slocum doubted the outlaw leader intended to do more than rest his weary packhorses. They hadn't even built a fire to brew coffee but instead passed around a quart bottle now only half full of whiskey.

"You're missin' out on the celebration," Jessup said, walking alongside them as they made their way down a steep embankment and into the ravine.

"How come you always get stuck with guard duty when the booze is bein' passed around?" Bench asked. "Seems your throat is as parched as theirs. And mine!"

Jessup laughed and escorted Slocum and Bench to where Turner had settled down. It didn't take a mind reader to see that Turner was not pleased to see them.

"Heard a lot of shots. Did you take care of the passengers the way I asked?"

"Good to see you, too, Turner," Slocum said. He dismounted and went to a spot near the closest horse with twin bags of gold coins slung over its back. He placed his hand on one bag, only to have Turner react as if he had shoved his hand into a fire.

"Get away from there." Turner reached for his six-shooter and Slocum backed off.

"When do we get our cut?"

"When I say, Slocum, and not an instant before."

Slocum eyed the canvas bags holding the coins and wondered why Turner had spun a story about this being army payroll. The bags were clearly marked as being from the Bank of Kansas City. If it had belonged to the army, they would have put their sigil on it the way they branded everything they thought was theirs.

"They wouldn't have gone along," Turner said.

"What's that?" Slocum saw Turner was answering the question that had boiled up in his mind when he read the words on the canvas sack.

"The boys. They wanted to believe we was goin' after army property. They wouldn't have taken kindly to stealing gold bein' used to buy homesteaders' plots by the damn railroad."

"Funny bunch of outlaws," Slocum said.

"Yeah, real funny."

Slocum knew Turner was still lying, but it hardly mattered. If Turner's lips were moving, he was lying. It was probably no more complicated than that. The men riding with him probably also wanted a share of revenge on the army, so that gave him added clout with them and Turner didn't run any extra risk of cavalry trotting out from behind their post walls, bugles blaring, to track him down. Yet.

"Where we heading?"

"You surely are filled with questions, aren't you?" Turner glared at him. "We'll be riding on in an hour. That ought to give the horses a rest and the men a chance to celebrate. Why don't you go help yourself to a swig of whiskey? It's a celebration."

Slocum wondered why Turner wasn't joining in, then discarded the notion when Jessup came up with a bottle and thrust it out for him. Slocum sampled it, nodded, and drank a bit more.

"Come on over and join us, Slocum. You and Bench are part of the gang now," Jessup said. Slocum followed the man to a spot where he could sit on a rock and occasionally partake of the bottle as it made its way around the circle of outlaws.

Two of the men were already roaring drunk and would pass out before long if they kept swilling the rotgut at the current rate. Slocum wondered if that was Turner's plan. Get the men drunk and steal all the gold for himself. More likely he would let them get drunk and then shoot the lot of them before riding away with the gold.

"You ever rob a bank?" Slocum asked Jessup.

"Never have. Been something of an expert on robbin' stagecoaches," Jessup said. "What you got in mind?"

"I wondered about the Bitter Creek robbery," Slocum said.

"Don't know nuthin' 'bout that," Jessup said. "The boss told us to steer clear of the town once we shot it up."

"Might be Turner or one of the others robbed the bank, then," Slocum said.

"Can't see they'd've had time. We been plannin' this robbery a long time. Leastways, the boss has. Took me by surprise when all we got from the wagon was dynamite. I thought *that* was the gold shipment."

"Anybody here have a grudge against the banker in Bitter Creek?"

"What are you askin' all those questions for, Slocum? Have some more popskull." Jessup shoved a quarter-full bottle at Slocum and watched him closely.

Slocum noticed that the bottle they had been drinking from was on the far side of camp. This one had appeared as if by magic. He put the bottle to his lips and kept from wincing at the way it burned. The potent brew never entered his mouth as he handed the bottle back to Jessup.

"That's powerful stuff," Slocum said, acting a little tipsy. He wondered if the bottle was poisoned or just had a Mickey Finn in it.

"No worse than the rest," Jessup said. "Hey, Bench, take a pull on this!" He tossed the bottle to Bench, who deftly caught it. Before Slocum could warn him, Bench had knocked back a finger's worth from the bottle.

The effect was almost immediate. Bench wobbled, belched, and started to say something. The words refused to come out, and he simply sat down where he was. His eyes glazed and then he slumped to the ground.

"More, Slocum?"

"Why the hell not?" Slocum said, aware that Turner and the rest were watching him like a hawk. Bench was still breathing. There was probably enough chloral hydrate in the whiskey to drop a bull buffalo. Slocum lifted the bottle, tilted it back, and took it into his mouth. He dropped the bottle so it smashed into fragments on a rock as he simply leaned back and flopped. He turned onto his side, spat out the drugged liquor, and lay still.

"He out?"

"Like the chamber pot first thing in the mornin'," said Jessup. "How come you wanted them drugged, boss?"

"Shut up. Get the horses saddled. We're movin' on right now."

"What about them?" Jessup asked.

"You shoot the pair of them when the sound won't scare the horses. You know how flighty the packhorses are."

"Seen how the one got spooked by the rattler," Jessup said.

Slocum peered up at him, lifting his eyelid the slightest bit. Jessup would shoot both him and Bench when Turner got far enough away. If Turner couldn't lose Jessup by hiding his trail, the outlaw would be the next one to be buzzard bait. One by one, Turner was getting rid of his gang.

"Then you know how long it would take to gentle them if they caught a fright from a gunshot," Turner said. "Take your time. Ain't no reason to hurry."

Turner clapped Jessup on the back. "I can count on you, Jessup, more than any of the others."

"I'll take care of them, boss. I will."

"There'll be that much more of the gold for each of us," Turner said. "When you've taken care of things, enjoy a snort out of my private stock. Here." He passed over a pint bottle to Jessup and finally disappeared from Slocum's limited field of vision. Horses whinnied and the sound of the rest of the gang leaving eventually faded. Jessup sat on a rock, working hard on the whiskey left for him by his boss.

Slocum watched closely to see what happened. It wasn't much of a surprise when Jessup half stood, looked around, and then tried to take a step. He tumbled facedown onto the ground. Turner had drugged him, too. Slocum wasted no time sitting up and getting his six-shooter out, ready for action in case Jessup wasn't out cold.

He knelt beside Jessup and pressed his fingers into the man's neck to check for a pulse. Slocum rolled him over and saw that Jessup was dead. Turner had poisoned him. He went cold inside when he realized that the other whiskey hadn't been laced just with knockout drops but with poison, too. Turner wasn't the sort to be subtle.

"Bench!" Slocum scooted to where his onetime partner had fallen. To his relief, Bench was still breathing raggedly. Then he saw what had saved the man from the poison. He had drunk heavily of the untainted liquor before taking the deadly bottle. When he had swallowed the poison, he had collapsed—and puked up everything in his belly. Neither Jessup nor Turner had noticed because Bench had fallen behind a rock.

"Wake up," Slocum said, shaking him. "Wake up!"

"Can't. Too tarred. Tarred 'n feathered. Damn good whiskey." Bench vomited some more. Slocum let him.

Slocum searched Jessup's pockets and took a few dollars in paper money and a silver coin. Not much legacy for a man who thought he was going to be rich after the train robbery. Slocum tucked the money into his vest pocket and went to see how Bench fared.

"Got a whole damn hive o' bees buzzin' in my head. My belly feels like a damn Apache knifed me. Whass goin' on, Slocum?"

"We have to ride. I doubt Turner will be back but he might. He tried to kill us both."

Bench didn't hear. He was busy losing the last dregs in his belly. Slocum got him to his feet, used the man's bandanna to clean him off, and then tossed it away. Supporting Bench, he got him to his horse. It took only a couple seconds for Slocum to decide Bench could never ride, so he boosted him up and over his saddle, belly down. As they rode away, the jostling against his midsection would take care of any poison remaining in him.

Slocum mounted and led Bench's horse with the semiconscious man across it up and out of the ravine. He wondered where to go, then realized there was only one place. Riding as fast as he could to outrace the approaching storm, Slocum headed for the Dahlquist farm.

13

"Quit moaning," Slocum said sharply. "You'd think you were going to die." The rain pelted down against the broad brim of his hat, sounding like it was hitting tin rather than felt. By keeping his face turned down, he kept the worst of the rain out of his face, but the intensity of the storm increased with every tired step his horse took.

"I feel like I am," Bench said. "I gotta sit up in the saddle. If I ride another foot like this, I'm gonna split in half. My belly's rubbin' up again my backbone and—"

"Ride if you can," Slocum said, drawing rein to wait for Bench to flop onto the muddy ground and then struggle into the saddle. From the way he weaved about, Bench was likely to take a spill at any instant.

He clung to the pommel with grim intensity. Slocum read the determination on the man's face not to fall off and humiliate himself further.

"Let's go."

"Where we headin'?"

"Someplace safe," Slocum said. He hoped the Dahlquist farm was a haven from both the weather and the outlaw gang. Since Turner had intended for Jessup to shoot both of them and then swill the poisoned liquor himself, he probably thought all three of them were dead. Slocum hoped so. Otherwise he'd have to spend the rest of his life looking over his shoulder, worrying that Turner or one of his gunmen would shoot him in the back.

"No place like that, not if Turner's after us."

"Shut up," Slocum said without rancor. He wanted nothing more than a dry space to sleep in. Warm would be good. And Laura beside him again would be even nicer, but he wasn't counting on that. Leaving her the way he had probably did more than put the frost on the pumpkin. She might come after him with that six-shooter Marcus waved around so foolishly.

"There's a sign. Farm," Bench said. "To hell with whose it is. I want to get dry once more before I die—and that's likely to be too damn soon."

Slocum almost cried out in triumph. The sign Bench had spotted marked the road to the Dahlquist farm. They had skirted Bitter Creek and come to the farm from the north. The short mile to the farmhouse stretched like eternity, but Slocum was glad to see a light burning in the front room window. In spite of the thunder and pounding rain, Marcus had heard them coming and stepped out on the porch, his pistol in his hand.

"Go away. We don't take kindly to thieves or beggars!"

"It's me, Slocum. All I want is to stay in the barn for the night."

"Who's that with you?" Marcus leveled the six-shooter, causing Slocum to reach for his. Shooting Laura and Cora's brother wasn't something he wanted to do, but he would if it looked as if either his or Bench's life hung in the balance. Marcus Dahlquist wasn't playing with a full deck any longer.

"John? Is that you, John?" Laura grabbed her brother's hand and pulled it down. The gun discharged, causing Bench to jump and Slocum to draw his hogleg.

"John!"

"You got him under control?" Slocum called out.

"What is this place? They're tryin' to cut us down so they obviously know you. Should we keep ridin'?"

"We're staying," Slocum said coldly. He rode for the barn, giving Laura time to deal with Marcus. Bench followed, ducking down as he rode into the barn. The leaks remained in the roof, but it was a mite drier inside than out in the gusty wind and rain.

"You surely do know a powerful lot of folks in these parts, Slocum. How many of them want to kill you?"

"Most all," he said, beginning to towel off his mare. Slocum fumed and fussed. He had hoped Marcus would have quieted down, but he clearly belonged in some kind of institution.

"John, you're back. I didn't know where you'd gone. I worried so!"

Slocum found himself clinging to Laura as she hugged him so tightly that it took away his breath. She pulled back and started to kiss him, then remembered Bench was there and watching intently.

"Not all of them want to shoot me," Slocum said. He introduced them, then saw Cora in the doorway. She came in almost shyly, her eyes fixed on Bench. Slocum introduced them, too, and then watched as Bench and Cora simply stood and stared at each other, not saying a word.

"Your friend," Laura whispered. "How long's he been on the trail?"

"Too long. I think Cora's gotten over Hop Franks."

"Might be, but she's been sulking around. This is the most alive I've seen her since you left." Reminding herself of Slocum's absence, Laura stamped her foot and demanded to know where he had been.

"I thought I could find out more about who killed the banker. It must have been Turner or one of his gang."

"Did they admit it?"

Slocum shook his head and sent water spraying about. Laura caught a drop in the eye, then shook her head in the same way, sending water flying, too. They laughed. Before Slocum could say anything more, she gripped his hand with feverish intensity and tugged him toward the rear of the barn.

"The bathhouse," she whispered in his ear. To make sure he got the message, as she turned she grabbed for his balls and gave them a squeeze. The last Slocum saw of her was her blushing face disappearing out into the storm.

"What brings you to Indian Territory?" Cora asked Bench. Bench looked over at Slocum for help. He wasn't about to tell the lovely woman what had drawn him to Bitter Creek.

"Joe is just passing through. We happened to run into each other in town," Slocum said.

"What do you do ... Joe?" Cora tried on the man's name like she might a pair of shoes. She wiggled around with it to see if it was too tight or too loose. From what Slocum could see, she found it just right. This made Bench a trifle uneasy, but he didn't back off as she inched closer to him until their bodies were almost touching.

"Same as me," Slocum said. "We worked together as cowpunchers, but Joe's a mighty decent farmhand, too." Slocum had no idea if Bench had ever done more than ride across a plowed field, but the answer pleased Cora and relieved Bench. That was good enough.

"Are you staying long?"

"I ... That depends on what Slocum intends. Me and him, well, we were partners a while back, and I thought we might ride together again. For a while."

"I'm sure Mr. Slocum's staying," Cora said. "I mean, he's worked here on the farm, helping us learn how to grow crops and tend the animals." Seeing Bench's startled expression, she asked, "You didn't know?"

Slocum edged toward the door as Cora and Bench began discovering what the other knew—and didn't. Bench was nobody's fool. He wouldn't go bragging to her about blowing up a train and robbing the gold shipment. Slocum worried he might touch his recent past with a bit too much color, but that was his worry. As he stepped into the storm, Slocum ran into Marcus Dahlquist.

"Why'd you come back? I asked in town and everyone said you'd left."

"Good to see you again, too, Marcus."

"I can make this farm profitable. I don't need you meddling. All you want is—"

"I wanted to find who murdered the banker."

Marcus tried to continue his rant, but the sudden change derailed him as surely as the dynamite had blown the train off its tracks.

"The banker?"

"I had a bargain struck with him to save the farm."

"I didn't approve that. You had no right! I can provide for my sisters. This is a good farm and my pa and ma made it that way. I can do even better. I don't need you or them. I don't need anyone to bring in a profitable crop!"

His voice turned shrill. In the flash of lightning, Slocum saw the madness on Marcus's face. Before a second lightning bolt lit up the land, Marcus had disappeared. Slocum looked around for him but couldn't see more than a dozen feet in the driving rain. Whether he had gone for his pa's six-gun to begin shooting up the place or had decided this was fine weather to weed the crops, Slocum didn't know. He was just glad that Marcus had left.

Slocum pulled his hat down low and walked into the teeth of the storm. The wind was fierce and the rain had turned cold. Every drop hitting his face stung like a bee. Instinct more than sight guided him to the bathhouse. He swung around and closed the door behind him. The roof didn't leak as it did in the barn. He had to laugh at the difference. What did it matter if the roof of a bathhouse leaked? Everyone came here to get wet anyway.

He leaned against the door when a particularly strong

gust tried to blow it open. Then he realized he was not alone. A lucifer flared and cast shadows all around before the candlewick ignited and gave off a dancing light. Laura snuffed out the lucifer. Shadows played across her in fascinating ways because her clothing was drenched and clung to her trim body like a second skin.

"I wondered if you would come," she said.

"Why wouldn't I?"

"You were leaving. I knew it. Marcus drove you off, but why did you return?"

"Marcus stopped me outside the barn just now. Has he been that way since I rode out?"

"He's better right now. If Cora and I agree with everything he says, he doesn't get violent."

"You should take the gun away from him and throw it in the stream. He's going to hurt somebody." Slocum didn't want either of the women hurt, but the notion of Marcus killing himself wasn't all that unsettling. It would solve a passel of problems for everyone involved.

"I've tried. He carries it with him all the time now," Laura said. She moved a little and began peeling her wet clothing away from her skin. The flickering candle turned her into an exotic, eerie, and entirely desirable figure.

"You don't want to stay on the farm, do you? That's Marcus talking." Slocum tried to concentrate on what he was saying, but it became increasingly difficult. Laura unbuttoned her blouse and slowly peeled it off her body to stand naked to the waist. The light cast shadows from her nipples and breasts and made every movement into something completely lewd, although he saw less than she revealed because of the darkness.

Laura instinctively knew what she was doing to him because she smiled, just a little, and turned slowly, hiding more of her torso and presenting her rump to him. She bent slowly to begin unbuttoning her shoes. Now and then as she moved her ass twitched.

What Slocum felt twitching wasn't his ass. He dropped his gun belt and began stripping off his soaked coat, vest, and shirt as he watched her swaying gently, as if every gust of wind outside moved her just a little. When she kicked off the second shoe, she half turned and presented him with her profile. The shadow bobbing on the wall made him entirely hard. He could hardly get free of his pants fast enough.

"You're overdressed," he told her.

"Oh? For what?"

"For what I'm going to do to you." He kicked free of his boots and pants and advanced toward her. Cold wind whipped through the bathhouse, chilling his flesh but doing nothing to bank the fires blazing in his loins. By the time he got around the galvanized tub between them, Laura had unfastened her skirt and dropped it in a heap around her ankles. The dancing candle flame hinted at more than it revealed, but Slocum knew what he wanted and where to find it.

Laura came into his arms, her cold breasts mashing flat against his chest. Their lips brushed, touched again tentatively, then crushed with a passionate kiss. He reached around and drew her closer, pulling her in to his body so that his hardness jutted between them.

"It's so cold, John," she said with a shiver.

"Let me slip something hot into you."

She gasped as he spun her about. She reached out and grabbed the high back of the galvanized tub. When he reached between her legs and stroked over her thighs, she understood what he intended. Laura widened her stance as he moved behind her, his manhood preceding him.

"Oh!" She gasped again as he bent his knees slightly, found the target, and then levered his hips forward. He sank an inch into her heated core. Two inches. More. She cried out as she rammed her hips backward to take him fully within her tightness.

For a moment Slocum stood and savored the feel all around him. His hands rested on her hips, holding her in place, but this wasn't good enough for her. She began moving back and forth, causing him to advance and retreat in the now-moist slit of her sex.

"You missed me," he said.

"I . . . I did. Every night I thought of you and it got worse and . . . Oh, John, oh! Fast. I need it fast!"

His hands gripped her waist and pulled her back into the circle of his groin as he pushed forward. For a few strokes it was awkward and then they both fell into the proper rhythm. She rotated her hips slightly as he started pistoning more powerfully. The wind howled outside, drowning out the woman's cries of stark desire.

They hung balanced like this, moving in their own private world, away from danger and worry, until Laura began trembling like a leaf in a high wind. Her movements turned ragged and she clutched down fiercely all around him. Slocum thought he had been caught in a mine collapse, but this wasn't rock but rather warm female flesh gripping him.

The fiery tides rose within him as he stroked faster. They once more found the right tempo and then the world exploded around them. Slocum pumped furiously and Laura screamed in release. As he went limp within her, she leaned forward against the tub for support.

"I need a bath," she said. "Hot water all around."

"I make you dirty?"

Laura laughed and said, "I want you in the tub with me. And yes, you make me feel dirty. Good dirty. Horny dirty. I want more of you, John. More!"

"I'm also making you greedy," he said. "I'm all tuckered out."

"I'd started the water outside. If the storm hasn't put out the fire, it ought to be ready. We can both carry in a bucket and that ought to be enough."

It was enough water for the bath but neither could get enough of the other's body until the storm began to abate near dawn.

14

Laura had barely returned to the farmhouse and Slocum had lain down to get what sleep he could when Joe Bench came into the barn, whistling off-key and looking like the cat that had eaten the canary. Slocum propped himself up on one elbow and said, "Knock that off. You're scaring the horses."

Bench whistled louder and flopped onto a pile of straw in the stall opposite Slocum's.

"I'm feelin' good. Real good."

"You and Cora?"

"Hey, nuthin' like that. I mean we sat up all night just talkin'."

"Is that what you call it now? Just talking?"

"You got it all wrong, Slocum. I didn't even kiss her. It just didn't seem . . . right. She's a real lady. I never met anybody like Cora."

Slocum heard the ring of truth in Bench's voice and marveled at it. When they had ridden together, Bench hadn't been too fussy about the women he bedded as long as it had been fast.

"Did she tell you about her brother?"

"Marcus? Yeah, she did. Cora thinks he is a little off in the head because his mood swings about so wild. One day he's sweet as plum wine and the next he's nuthin' but vinegar. Sounds to me that he's just got a powerful lot of responsibility on his shoulders that he's never had before."

"You're taking his part? That's one for the books," said Slocum.

"Not if he tries to hurt Cora," Bench said. The steel edge had returned and the whistling had stopped. Slocum knew Bench was definitely sweet on the woman, and from the way she had looked at him, he could tell Hop Franks was a distant memory for her.

Slocum had thought Cora had set her sights on Franks as a way to get away from her brother. But what was her game with Bench? He was as poor as a church mouse, and if she knew his background, she would avoid him like the plague.

"You tell her what you've been up to since coming to Bitter Creek?"

"No, and if you do, I'll cut your heart out."

"I'm not about to," Slocum assured him. "I'd have to mention what I've been up to, also."

"Right," said Bench. "I want to get some sleep. You can go on and do your chores. You got plenty of sleep last night, and my belly's still sore from all the puking I did back in that ravine. That son of a bitch is going to pay for tryin' to poison me the way he did."

Slocum didn't bother telling Bench he hadn't gotten any sleep either because he had spent the night with Laura. From the way Bench talked of his time with Cora, Slocum had the better of it.

"Need some more sleep," he said, his eyelids drooping. Slocum heard Bench say something about Cora, but he didn't care. He was too tired.

He came awake with a start, hand going for his six-shooter when Marcus banged open the barn door and let the afternoon sun stream in.

"He's back in town, and he's huntin' for you. Both of you!"

"Who's that?" Bench sat up, still more asleep than awake.

"That outlaw. Monty Turner."

"Turner's in Bitter Creek?" Slocum went cold inside. Turner had his gold and had probably killed off most of his gang to get a bigger take. Why would the outlaw return to Bitter Creek, even if he ruled it now that the town marshal had turned tail and run? It made no sense to Slocum, unless Turner had even bigger fish to fry than the gold shipment.

"He is. I saw him strutting around like the cock of the walk. He's a mean one," Marcus said.

"How many of his gang are with him?"

"A half dozen, maybe more. I didn't try counting them. You and Bench, you have to get out of Indian Territory or Turner will kill you for sure."

"Your concern is touching," Slocum said, not trying to hide his sarcasm. The instant the words left his mouth, Slocum regretted them. The light in Marcus's eyes changed to the insane glow that had been there when he and Bench had ridden up the night before. Marcus had been peaceful and reasonably sane until this moment. "I didn't mean anything by it," Slocum hastily said. He didn't want a fight with Marcus now. The gun butt protruding from Marcus's waistband convinced Slocum that would happen.

"You and Bench, you gotta run. Turner is after you."

Slocum thought hard on how Turner could have known the two of them were still alive. Unless he had returned and found Jessup dead, there was no way he could know. Why would Turner check on the three of them being dead?

"Was there a road agent named Jessup with Turner?" The only thing that made sense was that Jessup had somehow survived and gotten back to Turner with the tale of Slocum and Bench riding off. But Slocum was as sure as he could be that Jessup had drunk the poisoned whiskey and died.

"Might have been. Didn't go around introducin' myself to them. You and Bench have to skeedaddle."

"I'm not runnin' from a no-account like Monty Turner," Bench piped up. He had listened closely to everything Marcus and Slocum had said. "He don't scare me one little bit."

Slocum knew Bench's real motivation for standing his ground. Her name was Cora Dahlquist.

"He's right. We don't run. I never have and I never will." Slocum saw the craziness play across Marcus's face again. Where his senses came to rest was something Slocum couldn't determine. Marcus had a perfect poker face now, revealing nothing.

"You can hide out for a spell. The soldiers might run off the road agents."

"What soldiers?" Bench came over and looked as if he wanted to beat the information out of Marcus.

"There's an Injun uprising. Guess you didn't hear, you bein' gone and all," Marcus said. "Heard tell a lot of federal marshals and cavalry were comin' into Indian Territory. Lots more soldiers to put down the uprising." Marcus heaved a sigh, then said, "I got chores to do. You fellows just stay put and keep outta sight. You're gonna be fine, no matter there's outlaws and Injuns and cavalry all over the landscape."

Slocum watched Marcus leave, then turned to Bench and asked, "What do you make of that?"

"Crazy as a bedbug. Why would the Indians go on the warpath? That don't make sense. None at all."

Slocum had to agree. The Five Civilized Tribes were as peaceable as they came, being spread out all over the eastern part of Indian Territory on their tribal land. Occasional raiding parties of Arapaho and Sioux might drift down from the north but the Cherokee, Choctaw, Creek, and others who had been given this land were not likely to cause a ruckus that brought out more soldiers.

"He's trying to scare us off the farm," Slocum said.

"Why'd he want to do a thing like that?"

"I have my ideas, but the one thing he said that worries me is Turner coming back to Bitter Creek."

"That might be a fib, too," said Bench. "Ole Marcus, he don't have the look of a man who's always truthful."

"He might think he is, though," said Slocum. "Separating truth and lie is a chore for him."

"What are you going to do?"

Slocum heard the determination in Bench's tone. He was staying on the farm, no matter what his partner did.

"Is she worth dying for?" Slocum asked.

"Don't know what you mean," Bench said, looking away. "Cora's one fine woman. That's all."

Slocum laughed. He had seen men stick their heads in nooses for the love of a woman.

"Just be sure you know what you're doing," he cautioned. "I'm going to do some scouting in town. If Turner's back, everyone will know it."

"You be right careful, John. I'll stay here and keep the home fires burnin'."

"I'm sure Cora will give you a hand with that chore," Slocum said. He saddled and left without seeing Laura anywhere. As he rode away, Cora came from the farmhouse and hurried to the barn. She looked around furtively, then ducked inside to join Joe Bench. Slocum had to wonder what he had gotten himself into—him and Bench.

He approached Bitter Creek from the north to keep off the main east-west road running through the center of town. If Turner had come back, he would have sentries posted to alert him of travelers, whether they were sheep to be fleeced or the law to be avoided. It was late afternoon when Slocum tethered his horse out near the town bookstore. Slocum glanced inside the small shop but nobody was around. For his purposes, this was just fine. The fewer townspeople who saw him poking around, the fewer people who could tell Turner.

Slocum spun, dropped into a chair on the boardwalk in

front of the store, rocked back, and pulled his hat low to hide his face when two riders galloped down the main street. Slocum watched, trying to identify them as outlaws in Turner's gang. They might have been, but he could not say. They dismounted and went into the saloon, jostling one another and loudly insulting anyone nearby.

Waiting a few minutes to see if others joined them, Slocum took measure of the town. For late afternoon, Bitter Creek was strangely silent. No one walked the streets. The few horses tethered seemed to have permanently lost their owners. When he judged the two in the saloon had had time to knock back a couple shots, Slocum continued down the street and peered into the bank. The glass window had been shot out and boards nailed up, leaving cracks. Inside he saw the head teller and a female customer. Neither was in any hurry to complete her transaction. Slocum went in.

The teller jumped a foot when he saw Slocum.

"You're b-back," the teller stammered. The woman looked frightened, clutched at her purse, then bustled out after one final backward look.

"What's got the town so all fired scared?" Slocum asked.

"You don't know? Turner rode into town around noon with blood in his eye. He was asking for you by name, Mr. Slocum."

"Noon?" Slocum wondered how this was possible since Marcus had only told him and Bench of the outlaw's return then. Marcus had been in town during the early morning. "Are you sure that's when Turner came back to town?"

"He shot up the barbershop and Harry Niles—he's the owner—came over to complain how Turner ruined a clock. Bullet went smack through the mechanism. Froze it at a few minutes past noon." The teller's lips thinned. "Mr. Niles wanted a loan to replace that and other merchandise Turner destroyed but I had to tell him no."

"Still can't get into the safe?" Slocum looked past the teller to the heavy steel-walled vault.

"The combination died with Ernest Goodman. I've telegraphed the safe company in St. Louis on how to proceed but have not heard back from them yet."

"You can blow it," Slocum suggested. "Turner's got some dynamite left, I'd wager."

"D-dynamite? Turner?"

"Never mind," Slocum said. "Where can I find Turner?"

"Y-you'd hunt for him? To call him out?"

"If you tell me where he is, I don't have to hunt for him," Slocum pointed out.

"Down the street at the hotel. He took it over. Threw out all the customers and said it belonged to him now. Poor Mr. Sanborn's an old man and couldn't stand up to him."

"Obliged," Slocum said. "When you get that safe open and can get to the money inside, don't go taking it all. The townspeople need somebody they can trust. It might as well be you, as the new town banker."

"I don't know anything about that. I'm not really the bank owner. I have no idea who is, since Mr. Goodman had no family. He—"

Slocum left the teller babbling and stepped into the street. He had a tough decision to make. He could call out Turner or he could return to the farm so he and Bench could figure out what they wanted to do. With the outlaw's entire gang in Bitter Creek, facing him didn't seem like a smart move to Slocum.

He stepped back and tried to look inconspicuous when the two who had gone into the saloon came out, yelling and shoving and looking for trouble. The simple act of trying to get out of their line of sight drew unwanted attention.

"You, you there. The one with the stupid look. Git yer ass over here so we can have some fun!"

They came for Slocum. Both were so drunk that their eyes weren't focusing well enough to recognize him. When they got closer, there'd be no question who he was. He knew both of them, though not by name, and they weren't newcomers to Turner's gang. They had ridden into Bitter Creek with him before he had sent out the call for more guns that had drawn Bench to volunteer.

Slocum turned and walked away quickly, then cut down an alley and waited just around the corner, pistol drawn. Both road agents ran around the corner. Slocum shoved out his foot and tripped the first one. This distraction was enough for him to swing his pistol and catch the other just above the right eye. Slocum cursed his bad luck. Either the owlhoot had a thick skull or Slocum hadn't swung hard enough because the man yelped and grabbed his forehead. Blood spurted between his fingers but the volume and choice of cuss words convinced Slocum the man wasn't hurt all that bad.

"You're gonna die, you—" The outlaw went for his pistol. Slocum jammed his barrel hard into the man's gut, doubling him over. For a moment, Slocum almost tightened his trigger finger. At the last instant, he drew back, lifted his knee, and caught Turner's henchman under the chin. His head snapped back and he flopped to the ground, unconscious, as he should have been after Slocum had hit him in the head the first time.

The other outlaw struggled to hands and knees while fumbling for his six-shooter at the same time. Slocum judged the distance and launched a kick that ended in the man's midriff. His breath whooshed out and he collapsed. Slocum chanced a quick look into the street and was glad he hadn't fired or allowed either of them to. Turner and four more of his gang were calling out to get to their horses, undoubtedly wondering where these two varmints were.

Slocum kicked both of them for good measure, then hurried down the alley and made his way through the maze of Bitter Creek streets to his horse. He had found out what he needed to know and only a couple people had seen him. If Turner asked the bank teller, the man would spill his guts.

Otherwise, Slocum had drifted through town without leaving a trace.

He rode hard back to the farm, anxious to let Bench know that Marcus hadn't been blowing smoke up their asses and that Turner was on their trail. It still puzzled Slocum how Turner had known he and Bench were alive.

"John, you made good time. What'd you find out?" Bench looked around guiltily. Slocum guessed he had spent the entire time with Cora and not necessarily "just talking," as he had described their night together.

"We got all the trouble Marcus said and then some," Slocum told him, dismounting. "I can't say Turner's looking for us and nobody else, but he and the entire gang's in Bitter Creek."

"They spot you?"

Slocum shook his head. "The bank teller will spill his guts if Turner asks. I don't think he'd go to Turner on his own, though. He's afraid of his own shadow."

"Why'd you even talk to him? You got somethin' in mind?"

"The banker—Goodman—was shot in the back and robbed, but his vault wasn't blown. Only he knew the combination. The teller said he had telegraphed the safe company to figure out how to open it."

"So . . ." Bench said slowly, "you think there's money still in the safe?"

"Could be. We'd need a stake to move on. A stick or two of dynamite'd be all we would need."

"Can't say the money in that safe's doin' anybody a whit of good," Bench said, grinning ear to ear. "How much do you figure's in the safe?"

"Not as much as in the gold shipment Turner took," Slocum admitted. "But there'd only be the two of us splitting it."

"Yeah, two," Bench said, suddenly distant. Slocum knew the look and didn't like it.

"We could just hit the trail and forget about some extra money jingling in our pocket," Slocum said.

"There's that. Let's sleep on it, John. I need to do some hard thinkin' on the matter."

Slocum agreed and went to do what chores he could before the dark of night made any work too difficult. As he finished feeding the animals, Laura came from the farmhouse, looking distraught.

"Is it true? Cora told me that Turner and his gang were in town."

"It's true," Slocum said. He had wondered what Bench would do after learning of the outlaws riding so close. He had gone straight to Cora and Cora had told her sister. It was about what he had expected, though it still irked him a mite. Bench shouldn't have spread around the information until they had decided whether to leave or stay.

Slocum realized Bench had talked it over with Cora to make up his mind, and she had probably convinced him to stay. It was like that with a woman.

"We have to leave this place," Laura said. "There's no way we can make a go of it, even with you and Joe helping out. It's just too big a job for people who don't know about farming."

"Marcus wants to stay," Slocum said flatly.

"He thinks it would disgrace our parents' memory to sell out and go." She sighed deeply. "Who could we sell to? With Hop dead, our best chance of bringing in a crop is gone." She held up her hand before Slocum could speak. "You know farming. I can tell, John. But it's not what you want to do the rest of your life. It's not what *I* want to do now."

"Ride away. Leave it."

"Marcus has his heart set on it so."

"You coddle him too much. If he wants to prove the farm, let him. That doesn't mean you and Cora have to be here helping."

"I know, but—" Laura turned when the sound of a gal- loping horse echoed between the barn and house. "Who can that be?"

"Your brother, and from the look of it, he's mighty het up over something." Slocum made certain his six-gun rode loose in his holster, the leather thong that looped over the hammer slipped free.

"They're comin', they're on their way!" Marcus cried. "Not a mile down the road. Turner and all his gang. The lot of them found out you're here, Slocum."

"How'd they do that?" Laura asked.

"Must have been the bank teller living up to his title," Slocum said grimly. "You all get into the house. I'll see if I can't lure them off. Tell Bench."

"John, don't go. You can hide," Laura said, clinging to his arm. She released him when she saw his determination. Fighting Turner and his men was a fool's errand that would only lead to all their deaths. He had to decoy them away. The woman stared at him and tears welled in her eyes. "Go," she said in a choked voice.

"I'll be back," he promised, wondering if he would. At best he could lead the gang away. At worst he would finally become Turner's victim. If it came to that, he intended to take as many with him as possible.

He saddled and rode hard for the road, then kept going to circle into a wooded area a quarter mile from the farm where Turner had to pass by. A few shots might take out one or two of his gang and then lure the rest to chase him. Slocum concentrated hard on remembering the lay of the land. He had to use the terrain to his advantage, getting Turner separated from the others, causing them to split up and follow false trails. If he'd had a day to prepare, success would have been more likely.

Now all Slocum could hope for was to still be breathing come sunup.

After a few minutes, he grew uneasy. He hadn't asked

Marcus how far behind the outlaws were, but they should have ridden past by now. Slocum waited another few minutes and edged out of hiding to the darkened road. A sliver of waxing moon rose to give pale illumination—not enough to see far. He sat stock-still and listened hard. Only the normal nighttime sounds reached him. The drone of insects, the sporadic flash of lightning bugs, the smell of things growing—that was all he sensed until the shot rang out.

For a moment, Slocum couldn't determine which direction to turn. Then came a second, followed by four more.

"The farm!"

He raced back, his mare straining mightily as he retraced his route to the farmhouse. No light shone from the windows, but he hadn't expected there to be any if Bench was in charge. He knew how to fight in the daytime or during the nighttime.

Slocum hit the ground and ran a few steps before he recovered his balance. He vaulted up the steps and kicked in the door. Silence greeted him.

Drawing his six-shooter, he backed out and circled the house looking for any sign of Turner or his men. Nothing. He went back into the house and moved like a ghost from room to room.

In the kitchen he found her dead on the floor. She had been shot in the back.

15

Slocum searched the rest of the house but saw nothing out of the ordinary. Nothing had been broken or stolen, but the dead body on the kitchen floor gave mute testimony to the violence that had raged here only a few minutes earlier.

He heard a loud shout from the barnyard followed seconds later by the back door slamming open hard. He cocked his six-shooter and inched around, the barrel rising to come to rest on Joe Bench's chest.

"No," Bench cried, dropping to his knees. "Cora! You can't be dead. No!"

"What happened?" Slocum asked.

Bench whirled about so fast he fell heavily to the floor in his haste to aim his six-gun at Slocum.

"You killed her! Why'd you go and do a damned thing like that, Slocum?"

"I didn't shoot her. I just got back. Heard shots, rode hard," Slocum said as fast as he could. He didn't want to kill Bench but would if it looked as if the grief-stricken man would open fire on him. Slocum stayed partly hidden by the door frame as he watched the emotions play across Bench's face.

"Who did? Did you see who did?"

"Where were you?"

"Me and Laura were in the barn, huntin' for an old shotgun she said her pa kept there. I heard the shots, started for the house, and somebody hit me. I came to and found . . . Cora." He stared at the woman's lifeless body. Strangely, she looked composed in death, even pretty. Her pale cheeks were like porcelain now and her bright blue eyes were closed as if she only slept. The bullet that had shattered her spine left only a small red flower blossoming on her back, but there was no question she had died fast. She might not have even realized she was dead before she hit the floor.

"I didn't see anybody riding off," Slocum said. "I should have from the road. They must have headed out across the fields."

"I heard the shots. I couldn't save you," Bench said, putting his six-shooter on the floor and reaching out to touch Cora in such a way that he obviously hoped she would wake up and smile at him, favor him with a kiss or a hug.

Slocum went to the back door and looked out. The moon had drifted higher into the sky but failed to give much detail out back. A man could walk almost up to the house and never be noticed.

"Where's Laura?"

"I left her in the barn. I don't know what's become of Marcus. He sorta disappeared and I didn't much care."

Slocum slipped outside and again scouted around the house, hunting for tracks. The chickens had scratched up the dirt, but the few tracks he found didn't mean a whole lot. He hastily made his way to the barn, fearing what he would find there. With a swift kick, he opened the door and spun inside, six-shooter leveled and ready for action.

The cows mooed and made other bovine noises, complaining about being awakened. Slocum edged inside and moved through, checking each stall. Nothing seemed amiss—and he didn't see any trace of Laura Dahlquist.

He went to the bathhouse out back and pushed open the door with his pistol. His heart jumped into his throat when he saw a feminine hand dangling over the edge of the large galvanized tub. Slocum listened hard. Blundering into a trap would get him killed for sure. But he heard nothing but the faint whistle of wind through the sides of the bathhouse.

Two quick steps brought him to Laura's side. She lay fully clothed in the tub, her head lolled to one side. He cried out in joy when he saw a tiny trickle of blood from a scalp wound. Dead people didn't bleed.

"Laura, Laura!" He shook her until she stirred and moaned and her eyelids fluttered open.

"John? Where'd you go?"

"Tell me who hit you." He touched the gash on her temple. From the look of it, someone standing behind her had swung a pistol barrel and buffaloed her.

"Don't know. Didn't see. Marcus rode out, heard a shot, and started toward the house to find out what happened. Then—" She shook her head and groaned as new pain stabbed into her.

"Where'd Marcus go?"

"Thought he heard riders coming from across the field. I didn't hear anything, but he insisted on going to look."

She looked up at him and asked, "What's wrong, John? You're so grim."

"Cora's dead." It was best to simply let her know without any sugarcoating. Dancing around such bad news wouldn't do either of them any good when she finally realized her sister was gone.

"How?"

Slocum described how her sister had been gunned down from behind and finished by saying, "It must have been

Turner or one of his gang come for us. Marcus tried to warn me, but I missed them."

"I know you did your best, John. But Cora?" Laura burst out crying. Slocum held her until his shoulder was damp with her hot tears. "What do we do now?"

When Slocum didn't answer right away, Laura pushed back from him and looked into his eyes fiercely. "I want them dead. Whoever killed Cora like that doesn't deserve to live."

"The marshal left town," Slocum said.

"I know. I swear, I'll kill the killer myself. I'll get Marcus's six-shooter and do it!"

Slocum hesitated before saying, "Where is that gun? Still in the house?"

"Marcus has been carrying it with him, but I don't know. It could be. Why?"

Slocum returned to the house, avoiding the kitchen where Bench sat beside Cora, cursing steadily. Laura trailed but could not go to her fallen sister. The rolltop desk opened, and Slocum drew out the six-shooter Marcus was so fond of waving around. It was something of a puzzle that Marcus had left it in the drawer, but there it was. He took a whiff at the end of the barrel and knew it hadn't been fired recently. The gunpowder stench would linger for days if it had been. Even more curious, the gun was unloaded. He shoved the six-gun back into the drawer and closed it.

"Come on. We need to figure out how to deal with Turner." Laura resisted for a moment, then allowed herself to be pulled along into the kitchen. Bench looked up, eyes bloodshot. Slocum saw the faint wet tracks on the man's cheeks.

"Turner did this," Bench said. "The son of bitch ain't gonna get by with it."

"We can take care of him, but we'll have to do it together," Slocum said. "Him and his gang are murderers and outnumber us three or four to one. We—" That was as far as he got before Bench shot to his feet and shoved past.

"I'm gonna kill him. I swear, Slocum, I ain't never loved a woman like I did Cora, and Turner is gonna pay!"

Slocum started to go after Bench, but Laura grabbed him and slowed him.

"Let him go. I want Turner dead, too."

"Bench can't do it by himself unless he does like Turner and shoots him in the back. Bench is better than that." Before Slocum could disengage from Laura, the back door opened.

Marcus Dahlquist let out a gasp, then slammed the door behind him in rage.

"She's dead! My darling sister's dead!"

Laura and Marcus clung to each other, giving Slocum the chance to run after Bench. All he heard were receding hoofbeats. Bench had wasted no time getting on the road for Bitter Creek. Slocum thought Laura would be safe enough with her brother, and Bench needed his help. Together they would have quite a chore cutting down Turner. Barely had he reached the bottom of the front porch steps when Laura called out to him.

"John, wait. You have to!"

Reluctantly, Slocum turned and saw brother and sister standing close together.

"We need to bury her, Slocum. We have to. I want to do it on the ridge overlooking the fields where I buried my ma and pa."

"Do it," Slocum said.

"Please, John. I know what you meant to her. And I know what you, she, the two of you, what you did that first night. You owe it to her to see her laid to rest."

"I don't want Bench laid to rest, too."

"Turner probably didn't return straightaway to Bitter Creek," Marcus said. "See her buried, Slocum. She deserves that much."

Slocum fumed but went to the barn, grabbed a shovel, and followed Marcus and Laura across the field. Marcus carried his sister slung over his shoulder, stumbling as he hit the slope at the top of the ridge. Slocum began digging while Marcus and Laura stood over their sister. Laura had brought a blanket from the house and gently wrapped Cora in it while Slocum climbed from the grave he had dug.

"Could have been deeper," Marcus observed. He fell silent as Slocum glared at him. Marcus and Slocum lowered Cora as gently as possible. While Laura said words over her sister, Slocum shuffled his feet, anxious to get in the saddle and go after Bench. He saw the other two graves marked with crude wooden crosses where Marcus had buried his ma and pa. Slocum tried to put his finger on something that wasn't right, but nothing about the Dahlquist family seemed right to him at the moment.

As Laura finished, Slocum handed the shovel to Marcus and pointed. "Fill it in."

"John!" Laura ran after him and stopped him. He turned to tell her to stay with Marcus when she kissed him hard on the lips. "For luck," she said. Then she backed off, turned, and climbed the hill to stand beside Marcus as he struggled to complete his sister's burial. Slocum saw them outlined by the rising sun.

"And then there were two," he muttered. Slocum broke into a run to get to his horse. There would be one less if Bench ran afoul of Turner. Slocum wasn't sure he could do more than get himself shot up, too, but Bench was his partner. For better or worse, partners watched each other's backs.

Slocum got to Bitter Creek in jig time, expecting to see dead bodies scattered all over town. He rode slowly, hand near the butt of his gun in the cross-draw holster. There was no need to draw because nobody milled around in the street. He might have ridden into a ghost town.

He dropped off his horse at the bank and peered through

the boarded-up window. The lobby was as empty as a whore's promise. Slowly walking down the boardwalk, he looked in one store after another. Nothing. Nobody.

He knew the one place where he could find out what was going on had to be the saloon. Kicking back the door, he took a quick look around. He had been right about finally locating people. The barkeep cowered from him and tried to hide behind the bar.

"Where's everyone gone?" Slocum called. His words echoed in the empty room.

"Mister, they're all hidin', and you ought to, as well. Monty Turner's promised to bring down the wrath of hell on anybody crossin' him."

"Where is he?"

"Don't know. He rode out of town an hour back."

"A man came to town hunting for him. What did you tell him?"

"That galoot? Nuthin' since I don't know nuthin'."

Slocum stepped into the saloon and said, "Give me a beer." He leaned against the bar and, as the barkeep put the mug of thin beer on the counter, Slocum drew his Colt Navy and laid it so the muzzle pointed at the man's gut.

"You told Bench something or he'd be here waiting for Turner."

"Look, this ain't my fight. I—"

"It's mine. Turner killed Cora Dahlquist. Shot her in the back. I reckon he probably killed your banker, Goodman. Shot him in the back, too. This is my fight, and the man who was here earlier is my friend. What did you tell him?"

The barkeep turned pale and his hands shook as he nervously wiped them on the bar rag. His mouth opened. He snapped it shut, gathered his courage, and finally stammered, "Turner's just outside town. Him and his men looted 'bout everything they could and left. Said they was settin' up their own town."

"East of Bitter Creek?"

"Don't know but it must be. Said he was gonna be marshal and keep the federal marshals out."

"Why didn't he just move into Bitter Creek?"

"Mister, Turner don't tell nobody a thing. He plays his hand close to the vest."

"How long ago did you tell Bench where Turner was making his camp?"

"Couldn't have been more'n an hour. Less, maybe. I was a'feared of him, the way he roared through town, but he found me. I couldn't leave my saloon. This is all I got. The others can abandon their businesses but—"

Slocum was already out the door as the barkeep rattled on with his condemnation of the cowards who lived in Bitter Creek. From what Slocum had seen, they were the smart ones.

Smarter than him, since he was hunting down Monty Turner. He told himself it was to save Bench from getting himself killed, but it was more than that. Slocum had a score to settle with the outlaw leader.

16

Bench would end up dead if he didn't cool off before he faced Monty Turner. Slocum knew his friend well enough to know he kept a mad on for a long time. He was fiercely loyal, and with that came a fierce determination to get vengeance against anyone who wronged him. There was no question Turner had done that. Cora Dahlquist might have been the first woman Joe Bench had ever truly loved, and the outlaw had not only snatched her away from him, he had done it by shooting her in the back.

Slocum knew enough gunmen with reputations bordering on the legendary who never faced their opponent. A quick shot to the back proved safer than trusting to their speed and accuracy against someone who might be better. One notorious outlaw of Slocum's acquaintance had killed three men, all with a shot in the back. Slocum had seen one of the killings. The man's hand shook so badly he had to grip his six-shooter in both hands to even commit murder from behind.

Turner didn't have that problem, but he was a back-shooter nonetheless. If Bench hadn't gone after him, Slocum would have. The only difference lay in how Slocum would do it. Turner had a small army of cutthroats with him. Calling him out was likely to bring a hail of bullets from the others in his gang rather than getting the leader to come out and fight.

Slocum wasn't inclined to shoot a man in the back, but he would first cut him out of the herd before throwing down on him. Bench was likely to ride into the outlaws' camp with his six-gun blazing.

The road leading east was desolate and turned straighter by the minute until Slocum saw a good three miles into the distance. No rider kicked up a cloud of dust within sight. After the rains, there might not be much on the roadbed, but he should have seen some evidence of Bench or the outlaw gang if they had ridden in this direction.

"Whoa." He sat back and tugged on the reins to stop his mare. Slowly turning in a complete circle, he tried to find any trace of the outlaws or Bench. He had tried to keep an eye out for tracks leading away from the road, but the rain had scrubbed the ground clean of old hoofprints and made new ones difficult to see in mud puddles.

Slocum closed his eyes and inhaled deeply. He repeated this tactic four times before he caught the faint whiff of pine wood burning. With his eyes still closed he urged his horse in the direction of the odor and felt a soft, humid wind against his face. He approached a camp from downwind. When the savory scent of cooking meat reached his nose, he knew he was on the right trail—or some trail. Turner and his men weren't necessarily the only ones out on the prairie right now. There might be companies of cavalry or even the Indians that Marcus had gone on about. That seemed less likely than encountering soldiers and even less likely than him riding toward Turner's camp.

Knowing how Turner posted sentries who remained alert, Slocum dismounted some distance away and approached on foot. He moved quietly through the lightly forested area until he found a stream meandering down into a shallow bowl of a valley from where the cooking odors rose. He hunkered down and waited to see if any unusual activity had been sparked in camp.

If there had been, it probably meant Bench was dead.

After ten minutes, he heard only faint sounds of the outlaws moving around, the click of knives against tin plates and the occasional curse as the men jostled one another. Only then did he begin moving slowly, creeping more than walking, until he found a spot looking down on Turner and his men.

The outlaw leader stood to one side of the camp, arguing with a man facing away from Slocum. By now, Slocum thought he could recognize most of the outlaws, but this one might be a new recruit. Slocum went for his six-shooter when Turner shoved the man backward. Stumbling, the outlaw went for his pistol but Turner hit leather fast, drew, and fired point-blank into the man's chest. From the way he crashed onto the ground, Slocum could tell he was dead before he hit.

"Nothing to get het up over, boys," Turner called. "This son of a bitch wanted more than his fair share."

"That just leaves more for the rest of us," came a cry from somewhere in the camp. Others picked up the slogan, and they began laughing and playfully shoving each other.

Slocum wondered if they realized how Turner was reducing their number until only he would be left. Why he had stuck around after the gold shipment robbery was a question Slocum would like answered—but he wanted the outlaw dead more than he needed to satisfy his curiosity.

The gunshot did more than kill the argumentative outlaw. It caused movement in the forest to Slocum's left. At first he thought it might be a sentry. Then he saw Joe Bench moving purposefully, a rifle clutched in his hands. Slocum waved, hissed, and tried to get his friend's attention, but

Bench was too intent on the camp and his target—Monty Turner.

As he moved closer for the shot, he neglected to look behind him. An outlaw crept up, got a good look to see that Bench wasn't one of the gang, and then drew a bead on the man's back. Slocum never considered the trouble he would cause as he drew and fired in a smooth motion. His slug hit a branch and deflected, but he still winged the outlaw. The man yelped like a stuck pig and grabbed for his right forearm where Slocum's bullet had pinked him.

Bench might have been hunting Turner but he knew enough to freeze, then drop, roll, and come up facing the outlaw with his rifle pointed at the man.

"Move and you're a dead man," Bench said in a raspy voice.

Slocum wasted no time closing the distance between them. The outlaw might have tried to dodge Bench's bullet, but when he saw that Slocum had him in a cross fire, he dropped his rifle and raised his hands.

"We got ourselves a prisoner, John," Bench said. "Ain't the one I want, though."

"You can't get away with this," their prisoner said. "Turner will cut out your hearts and eat them!"

"You won't care a whit 'cuz you'll be dead," Bench said. "That way!" He indicated a small clearing directly behind the outlaw, well away from the camp in the valley below.

"You gonna kill me?"

"I had the chance," Slocum said.

"You mighta missed."

"He's the best damned shot you'll ever find west of the Mississippi," Bench said. "If he winged you, he meant to. If he'd meant to spatter your brains all over the ground, you'd be huntin' them with both hands right about now."

The man was unconvinced by that argument, but the sight of two weapons unwaveringly pointed at him caused him to obey.

"Fancy you showin' up just when I needed you, John."

"You couldn't handle Turner alone. He's got too many guns backing him up."

"Like this one?" Bench laughed, and it was short and ugly. "I'm gonna kick his ass all the way into a shallow grave for what he done to Cora."

"You intend to shoot me, don't you?" their prisoner called.

"Keep your voice down," Bench snapped. "We'd have cut your dirty throat by now if that was our intention." In a whisper, he asked Slocum, "Why *are* we keepin' 'im alive? I want 'em all dead."

"I want answers first."

"Yeah, right, I forget. The gold." Bench glowered. "You know, John, it don't matter so much to me. Not as much as revenge for Cora's killing."

"This one might know who pulled the trigger," Slocum pointed out.

"That don't matter to me. Turner's the boss, he gets killed no matter what. I'll take the rest of 'em with me, if necessary, but somebody's got to pay for her death. I loved that woman, John, I truly did."

"Sit there," Slocum ordered their prisoner. "Back against the pine tree."

The outlaw spiraled down and pressed his back to the tree trunk. He glared at the two men.

"We can make this easy or you can make it hard," Slocum said. "Don't answer and you will feel an awful lot of pain." He drew the thick-bladed knife he carried in the top of his right boot. "I rode with Apaches for damned near six months and saw what they did to their prisoners. Wasn't pretty."

"That one fellow took three days to die, but we don't have that much time," Bench said, playing along.

The outlaw tried to scream, but Slocum moved too fast to allow it. He clamped a hand over the man's mouth, then tipped his head back and pressed the sharp edge of his knife against the agitated, bobbing Adam's apple.

"One peep out of you and you'll be smiling with a second mouth."

"Why not? You're gonna kill me anyway."

"We want Turner," Slocum said.

"I want the one who killed Cora!" Bench hopped up, shoved his six-shooter into the man's face, and drew back the hammer. If Slocum's knife hadn't convinced the outlaw they meant business, the expression on Bench's face did.

"What woman? Who you talkin' about?"

"Lying's not gonna save you, if you know who killed her."

"I could tell you it was Turner, but I just don't know," the man said.

"Did you go out to a farm west of town and kill a woman there?" Slocum asked. He watched the fright mounting on the man's face. Some of it came from the nearness of the knife and the pistol, but a greater part came from not knowing. He wanted to give them the name of the killer but didn't have any idea who it was.

"Don't know about no farm."

"Goodman, the banker. Who shot him?"

"None of us. We stayed out of town 'cept when Turner was with us. He's worried that the townspeople would get some backbone and form a vigilance committee. He's got plans, and bein' chased around by a bunch of old men with shotguns ain't part of them."

"Cora," insisted Bench, but Slocum motioned his friend back.

"What's Turner up to? He scored big with the train robbery. Why's he sticking around?"

"He's got it in for the railroad. The owner done him wrong, and he wants to punish him for somethin'. Honest, I don't know what went on between 'em. The more Turner can steal, the more he can make him look bad, the sooner the railroad goes bankrupt."

"What'd he do with the gold?" Bench asked in a low voice that was almost pleading.

"Hid it. Won't tell us where. That's why most of us are stayin' with him. We want our cut. He said all we need to do is rob a couple more trains and he'll pay us off."

"You believe him? A backshootin' son of a bitch like Turner? You believe him?"

The man shrugged. "Reckon so. He hasn't treated us all that bad."

"You don't know anybody who rode to the Dahlquist farm and shot a woman in the back?" Slocum held Bench back as he asked. The outlaw was opening up. He was likely to tell them what they needed to know if he wasn't frightened out of his wits.

"None of us. We ain't even been in town, most of us. Turner's been out scoutin' where to rob the next train. He heard they're sendin' along a freight car full of federal marshals, and he knows how to decoy them away so he can rob the train again. That's all I know. What he's up to is somethin' only him and God know."

"Him and the devil," grumbled Bench. He stepped back. He had heard the truth in the man's words, just as Slocum had.

"What you gonna do with me? I told you everything I know. Honest!"

"You haven't been honest in so long, you don't I know the meaning of the word," Slocum said. He looked over his shoulder and then half turned when he saw that Bench had vanished. This was all the opportunity the outlaw needed. He surged forward, arms circling Slocum's waist. A bony shoulder in his gut drove Slocum back until he caught his heel on a rock and tumbled down hard. His knife went flying and the outlaw was on top of him, pummeling him with clumsy punches and trying his best to knock Slocum out—or kill him with his bare hands.

Slocum arched his back but couldn't budge the man, so

he reversed direction, grabbed a handful of shirt, and pulled. The outlaw crashed to the ground. Slocum kicked, then got his feet under himself and drew his six-shooter in a lightning-fast move. He swung the barrel and clobbered the man on the top of his head.

The outlaw went down as if Slocum had turned all his bones to water.

Panting, Slocum stood over him a moment to catch his breath, then ran after Bench. With Cora dead, Bench thought his life meant nothing. Slocum didn't want him dead—and he didn't want Bench doing anything that would cause him to end up dead, too.

If Bench had stirred up the den of rattlers gathered around the campfire, Slocum didn't want to step right into the rattling, wiggling, deadly mass of outlaws. He skirted the camp and came up in a different direction in time to see Bench walk around the edge of the encampment in plain sight, as bold as brass. The outlaws paid him no heed since they were engaged in a poker game.

Slocum saw right away what Bench already had. Turner had left the camp and was walking into the woods opposite. He considered his chances of duplicating Bench's brash behavior and knew he would never make it. Slocum faded back into the trees and made his way through the underbrush as quietly as he could, giving the outlaws a wide berth.

By the time he came upon Turner taking a leak, Bench had already positioned himself. His friend sighted along the barrel of his six-gun, ready to shoot the outlaw leader in the back.

Slocum reached out and clamped his hand down between the hammer and the firing pin just as Bench squeezed the trigger. Slocum tried to hold back the yelp of pain as the hammer cut into the web of skin between his thumb and index finger and failed. The sound, along with the commotion they made as they scuffled, alerted Monty Turner. He looked around from doing his business and cried out.

Still hanging out, he went for his six-shooter. Slocum clamped his fingers around Bench's gun and flung it at the outlaw as hard as he could. Flesh tore and blood spurted from his hand, but Slocum's aim was accurate enough to get Turner off balance for an instant.

Both Slocum and Bench swarmed over him, Bench grabbing the outlaw's throat to keep him from crying out and Slocum kicking his feet out from under him. The trio crashed to the ground.

"Stop strangling him," Slocum rasped out. The pain in his hand spread all the way up into his forearm. Using his own six-shooter was going to be a chore until the torn flesh healed.

"I want him dead. He killed Cora!"

"What if he didn't? What if one of his men did? You'd be letting her murderer go scot-free."

"Then I'll have to gun them all down. Somebody's got to pay for shooting her in the back." Bench leaned forward to press his entire weight into the two-handed choke hold around Turner's throat.

"Find out for certain. Turner knows. If he did it, he's the kind who'd brag about it." The words penetrated Bench's thick skull. He leaned back and eased up on the pressure. Turner gasped and began coughing.

"You want to ever breathe again, you'll tell me what I need to know," Bench said. Turner glared at him.

"I'm never gonna tell you where the loot is."

"Screw the gold!" Bench cried. "Did you shoot Cora?"

"Who?"

"You went out to the farm and you shot her in the back. Admit it!"

"I don't know what you're talkin' about," Turner said. His voice came out in a hoarse whisper that ended in a gurgle when Bench began squeezing the life from him again.

Slocum laid a bloody hand on Bench's arm. "Let him talk some more. I got questions."

"I told you, I don't care about no damned gold. He murdered the woman I loved! And she loved me!"

Slocum watched Turner's expression and felt his stomach knotting up. Turner didn't know any more about Cora Dahlquist's death than his henchman had.

"What about the banker in Bitter Creek?" Slocum asked, still watching Turner closely. "Did you kill him?"

"No, but I wish I had. He was agitatin' to hire a new marshal after I ran off the old one. He thought he was some kind of authority for the town. I couldn't let that stand, but I didn't kill him. Somebody else did that for me."

"Why didn't you go back into town?" Slocum asked.

"The people was all pissed at how we shot up the place. They started snipin' at us. I coulda burned the whole damned town to the ground but I have bigger fish to fry."

"The owner of the railroad," Slocum said. The surprise on the outlaw's face convinced Slocum he had hit on the truth. "You want to ruin him."

"The son of a bitch had my brother hanged for no good reason. And he swore out a warrant with Judge Parker when I didn't do nuthin' at all. Well, I'm gettin' even with him. I'm gonna pluck the entire Indian Territory clean and make sure not a single locomotive crosses this stretch of worthless prairie."

"Who cares?" Bench leaned forward again to strangle his prisoner but Turner grabbed his wrist and twisted hard, unseating Bench. He slammed into a tree and was momentarily stunned.

Slocum went for his Colt, but the blood on his hand made the butt slippery. He got off a wild shot that missed by a country mile. From the direction of the outlaw camp came angry voices.

"We got to get out of here," Slocum said, shaking Bench until he got his senses back.

"You let him go! You let that murderin' swine get away!"

"We're both dead if we try to catch him now," Slocum

said. "Between you shouting about the gold and me missing, we've stirred up a hornet's nest."

"I'll kill him. I don't care what that liar says, he killed Cora."

"Come on," Slocum said urgently. He grabbed Bench's arm. "Let him go for now. We've got to stay alive so we can track him down later."

"You let him go," Bench growled, but he followed Slocum into the forest. They had a powerful lot of work ahead of them if they wanted to avoid the rest of Turner's gang.

17

"They'll cut us off if we try going that way," Slocum called to Joe Bench. "The ravine twists around in an oxbow. We don't want to be at the bottom."

"They'll see us if we don't get walls on either side of us." Bench grumbled and then added, "We wouldn't be in this pickle if you hadn't let Turner go. The murderin'—" Bench ducked when angry bullets whined past his head.

Slocum bent low and cut sharply to the right. After a dozen strides, the horse veered left and then back right. The slugs passed harmlessly into the night. He presented too small and fleet-footed a target.

"Bench!" Slocum cut back again and hunted for his friend. He saw a puff of dust and then heard only the pounding hoofbeats as Bench raced down the ravine. He was like a cow in a chute and could only go in one direction now. If any of the outlaws had a faster horse, Bench would be buzzard bait.

Slocum zigzagged back and galloped along the brink of the ravine, careful not to get too close, fearing the soft earth would crumble under him.

"Bench, get out of there!"

Slocum realized his mistake instantly. He had drawn away attention from the outlaws on Bench's tail. The bullets that had sailed harmlessly through the air before now homed in on him. Slocum had no choice but to cut back and away from the ravine, leaving Bench to his own devices. Riding hard, Slocum put a mile between him and the outlaws before slowing to give his mare a rest.

He fumed as he walked along, turning over everything in his head. He owed Bench for what he had done. It riled him something fierce, but Bench was right. He had let Turner get away. Even if Turner wasn't responsible for Cora's death, he had enough blood on his hands to make him a worthy guest of honor at a necktie party.

Turner's blood feud against the owner of the railroad gave Slocum the idea how to get back at the outlaw. Where the gold shipment might be hidden was something he might never know, but he could square things with Bench by getting rid of Monty Turner. He doubted Bench cared much how this end came about.

Slocum angled away from the road and headed across country, up hills and down into shallow valleys that filled with morning mist as the sun rose. By the time he crossed the railroad tracks, he had figured out where he rode. Turning westward, he trotted alongside the tracks until he came to a way station. A quick glance up convinced him this was the right spot. Telegraph wires not only followed the railroad tracks, they also split off and went north and south.

"Howdy, mister. You wantin' a ticket? East or west?"

"I need to send a telegram," Slocum said.

"We kin do that, too. Which direction?"

"What's the best direction to bring some railroad detectives down on Monty Turner's head?"

The stationmaster turned wary. He reached under the counter but did not bring out whatever he had hidden there.

Slocum figured it had to be a sawed-off shotgun. Out here in the middle of nowhere, anything less would be useless.

"What do you know of Turner?"

"He robbed the train of a big gold shipment and he's sworn vengeance on the road's owner. He wants to bankrupt him. Mr. Gibbons saw Turner's brother put into custody over at Fort Smith. Judge Parker stretched his neck and that started the feud."

"I don't much care for the details. Turner has vowed to rob every stagecoach and train in this part of Indian Territory. That might make sending for the cavalry a better choice."

"Or maybe the federal deputies. They're out of Fort Smith and responsible for keepin' the peace. Not that they can keep up with the crime. This is mighty wide-open range for only a handful of men to patrol."

"I know exactly where Turner is camped," Slocum said. "That ought to entice somebody out. Who's the most likely to capture him?"

"Not the railroad dicks, that's for certain sure," the station agent said, shaking his head. "If Gibbons sent them out, their orders would be to gun down Turner on sight. That bother you none?"

"Nope," Slocum said. "Why don't you send telegrams to the army, to the railroad's main office, and to the federal marshal? Somebody's bound to carve a notch for Monty Turner in his pistol butt if they all come hunting for him."

"You surely do have a hatred for him, don't you? What'd he do to you?"

"He killed a friend's lady love," Slocum said. "He shot a banker over in Bitter Creek in the back. More than once he tried to kill me."

"You got cause to want him dead, then. I'll send the 'gram to Mr. Gibbons, his eyes only."

"Doesn't matter. If you send it open, word'll get around and that will guarantee somebody coming after Turner and his gang." Slocum detailed where he had seen the outlaw camp and gave suggestions as to where Turner was likely to move. The station agent listened in silence, then fetched a map and traced out all Slocum had said.

"You sure of where he's camped?"

"As of last night," Slocum said, finger stabbing down on the valley where the road agents had camped.

"He won't stray far, then. He can ride down this valley and be at the railroad tracks inside an hour. There's another shipment comin' . . ." The stationmaster looked up sharply. "Can't say too much about that since nobody's supposed to know."

"Turner seems to or he wouldn't be camped so close. Might be he has someone in Gibbons's office feeding him the information."

"All the more reason to send the 'gram for Mr. Gibbons's attention only," the man said. "There's likely to be a huge reward, as much as a hundred dollars for bringin' down Monty Turner."

"It's yours. I'm doing this for friends."

"You're doing it to get even with him. Is revenge so sweet that you'd pass up that much money?"

Slocum smiled grimly and nodded. It was.

The stationmaster had let Slocum keep the map. He held the corners down with rocks as he moved around to orient himself. Letting Bench fend for himself didn't seem like too smart a thing to do. The man was going on suicidal and might take it into his head to attack the entire gang. If he did, he was already dead, but Slocum hoped Bench had kept a measure of control so he could personally put a bullet or two in Turner.

Finally deciding where Bench was most likely to have gone if he had followed the ravine very far, Slocum cut across the countryside, making as good a time as he could. It was just before sundown when he found something that made him dismount, drop to one knee, and puzzle over the tracks.

Bench had a half dozen of Turner's gang on his tail, but these tracks showed something entirely different happening. Bench had ridden along the ravine and there hadn't been tracks following for more than five miles. He had outdistanced Turner's men, or possibly the outlaw leader had called them back, figuring Bench was no threat to them.

Bench had ridden along the ravine bottom but two riders had approached him, one from each side, to catch him in the jaws of a vise. The outlaws couldn't have gotten ahead of Bench without killing their horses. Everything pointed to them quitting the chase along the bottom of the wash, so who were the two that trapped Bench?

Slocum followed three sets of tracks away. Bench rode in the middle with the newcomers on either side. As far as he followed on foot, they didn't change the order, no matter how rocky or sandy the ravine bottom.

"Lawmen," Slocum said softly. Bench had ridden into a trap laid by lawmen. In this part of Indian Territory that meant federal deputies from Fort Smith. "They're taking a prisoner back to Judge Parker."

Slocum heaved a sigh and shook his head. Bench had a black cloud following him no matter where he went, raining down on his head constantly. Slocum had done what he could to stop Turner, but tangling with deputies accustomed to riding this territory wasn't something he wanted to do for Bench.

But he had no choice. Isaac Parker had issued "suspended sentences" for more than a hundred men and bragged on how he was going to hang two hundred. Slocum didn't want Joe Bench to help the judge toward his goal.

He swung into the saddle and, in spite of his mare being exhausted, pressed on into the night. His perseverance paid off just before dawn when he saw the light from a small campfire ahead. He had found the deputies and their prisoner, but what did he do now?

There wasn't any way he could ever hope to outride the peace officers, not on a mare so tired it stumbled along. He had to do something else, and if he killed the deputies, there would be a hue and cry raised for him that wouldn't end at the edge of Indian Territory. The "Wanted" posters would circulate everywhere in the West. He had more than one dogging his steps, but nothing like one a determined Judge Parker would issue. If a big reward was put on his head, bounty hunters from all over would flock after him.

Bench was his friend, but Slocum wasn't about to die for him if there was some other way to get him free.

When he paused a moment, a deputy noticed him and reached for his rifle. Slocum knew the fat was in the fire.

He urged his tired horse forward and called out, "You gents lawmen? You got here mighty fast."

"What are you goin' on about?" said the one holding the rifle. The other rested his hand on his holstered six-shooter but did not draw. On the far side of the fire Bench lay with shackles on his feet. Slocum couldn't see his hands but thought they were shackled, also.

Slocum rode closer and put the two deputies on guard.

"I had the stationmaster send a telegram to Fort Smith about Monty Turner. He's going to rob another train. Has a real thing about the road owner, a man by the name of Gibbons." Using the railroad owner's name put the two deputies more at ease.

"We didn't come for Turner, but we heard about him. The judge hanged his brother a while back."

"I heard tell that's what got Turner all het up. He wants revenge on Gibbons and wants to drive the railroad bankrupt by robbing every single last train rolling across Indian Territory."

"He'll have a chore ahead of him, then. There are dozens of trains, all owned by Gibbons," said the second deputy. "You want some coffee?"

"That's mighty generous," Slocum said. "But you aren't on Turner's trail?"

"We got ourselves another desperado," the deputy with the rifle said. He did not lower his weapon but kept it pointed in Slocum's direction. "This one's got a fifty-dollar reward on his head."

"Doesn't look like an outlaw," Slocum said, dismounting. "What's he supposed to have done?"

"He—" This was as far as the deputy with the rifle got. He half turned to look at Bench and gave Slocum the opening he needed. The instant the rifle barrel was no longer trained on him, Slocum moved like a striking snake. He grabbed the rifle barrel and yanked hard. He winced when the deputy fired. The suddenly hot barrel burned the web on his hand that he had injured keeping Bench from gunning down Turner. Slocum ignored the pain, stepped closer, and twisted the rifle from the lawman's hands.

For a moment they stood staring at each other. The deputy shook himself free of the spell, grabbed for his six-gun, and was rewarded with his own rifle stock slamming into the side of his head. He dropped to his knees, groaning.

"Freeze, mister," said the other deputy. He had his six-shooter out and pointed directly at Slocum. Then he pitched forward and crashed facedown on the ground.

Bench had rolled over and kicked hard at the back of the deputy's knees with one foot as he wrapped the chain from the other foot in front. By tangling the lawman's feet, he effectively tripped him.

Slocum took another swing at the deputy on his knees beside him and knocked him out. Only then did he tend to the struggling lawman Bench fought to keep pinned to the ground.

Just as the deputy wiggled free, he found himself staring down the barrel of Slocum's gun.

"I'll shoot if I have to," Slocum said. The deputy stared into cold green eyes and knew Slocum meant it.

"You'll hang. The pair of you! Judge Parker'll laugh as he raps his gavel and announces your sentences!"

"Don't know about that," Slocum said. "But I do know it's not too smart of you to shoot off your mouth when you're looking down another man's gun barrel."

"And the one holding the gun's the varmint you just promised to hang," Bench chimed in. "Didn't think I'd ever see you again, John."

"I thought Turner had caught you."

"Outran that son of a bitch. Then I blundered into an ambush these two set."

Slocum nodded. He had figured this out easily enough from the hoofprints in the ravine bottom. Everything they said the deputy took in. Slocum didn't doubt the deputy would remember every detail and relate it if either of them ever went to trial in front of Judge Parker. That wasn't going to happen if Slocum had anything to do with it.

"Where's the key to his shackles?" Slocum stared hard at the deputy Bench had tripped. The furtive glance downward told him what he needed. "He's got the key in his left vest pocket," Slocum told Bench. "Get it while I keep him covered."

The deputy was smart enough to know that Slocum couldn't miss if he fired and didn't try anything. Bench plucked the key out and unfastened his shackles. He started to throw them away but Slocum stopped him.

"Chain them together," Slocum told Bench.

"What then?" Bench asked.

"We'll use both sets of shackles on their ankles and leave their hands free."

"Why'd we want to do a thing like that? I say chain them around a tree."

The deputy said nothing but watched Bench and Slocum argue his fate.

"They might not be able to get free," Slocum said. "There's no call to kill them if nobody comes along to free them. This way they can't walk, but a few hours of work hammering at the locks with a rock will get them free."

"We'll come after you," the deputy said. "I ain't sayin' anything that's not already rattlin' around inside your schemin' head."

"You'll have to do it on foot. We're taking your horses. Mine's all tuckered out."

"With two horses, we can swap off and get twice as far in half the time," Bench said, chuckling. "Which way do we ride, John?"

"No sense letting them know. We can ride out of here, then circle around and head whatever way we want. As you said, we can be fifty miles away from here by sundown."

"In some unknown direction—unknown to them. What do you think Judge Parker's likely to do to them for losin' a prisoner—and their own horses?"

"That depends on what they tell him," Slocum said. He saw the calculation behind the deputy's eyes and knew a whopper of a lie would be given to the judge and his court officers. That saved the deputies' reputations and probably kept the judge from finding them in contempt of court for losing a prisoner.

Bench whistled as he chained the two lawmen together. He saddled their horses and sat waiting for Slocum.

Slocum rode one of the deputy's horses to rest his own mare. He backtracked on the trail that had led him to Bench and drew rein when they were out of sight of the deputies.

"You goin' back to the farm?" Bench asked. His voice was barely a whisper. "I don't think I can do that. It'd remind me of Cora. I got to go after Turner."

"What I said about getting the railroad detectives after him was the truth," Slocum said. "If he doesn't leave Indian Territory right away, he's going to find himself strung up from a tree limb. Whoever Gibbons sends after him, Pinkertons or his own private guards, won't matter."

"You passed along where his camp is? You know there's not a chance in hell of finding the gold he stole if he gets arrested—or hanged."

Slocum shrugged.

"I'm ridin' on, John. I can't say it's all been skittles and beer, but it has been good ridin' with you again." Bench thrust out his hand. Slocum shook.

"Any time our paths cross again," Slocum said, "you've got a partner, if you want one."

"Partners," Bench agreed. He nodded to Slocum, then put his heels to his horse's flanks and galloped southward. Slocum knew Bench might kill one of the horses under him before he reached the Red River, but he would put more miles between him and the judge's deputies.

Slocum didn't wait for Bench to ride out of sight before heading directly west, on the trail again to the farm—and Laura Dahlquist.

18

Slocum looked up the road toward the Dahlquist farm. No one stirred but chickens in the yard, and a milk cow penned up behind the barn showed someone had taken care of feeding earlier in the morning. He walked his mare slowly toward the house and looked around. Other than the usual animal sounds, the area was quiet. Almost too quiet, since it got on his nerves. He relied on sound as much as sight to warn him of danger.

Silence often meant more trouble than he could handle.

He dismounted and went into the house.

"Anybody home?" Slocum went from room to room but the place was deserted. For a moment he thought—hoped—that Laura had decided to go back to St. Louis where she belonged. There was nothing for her on a farm outside a miserable little town in the eastern end of Indian Territory. It was her brother's dream, not hers, that kept them scrabbling in the dirt and thinking crops would grow by themselves.

"Laura?" He went into her bedroom. The bed was neatly made and the curtains pulled back to let in both light and the breeze fitfully blowing across the fields. A quick check of the wardrobe showed her clothing still hung and her spare pair of shoes neatly lined up on the floorboard.

He went outside, slipped the leather thong off the hammer of his six-shooter, and started looking for her. He had seen nothing to tell him that Marcus had hightailed it, but if he had, Laura wouldn't be far behind. Slocum worried that Turner and his gang had somehow swept back past here and caught both of them in a deadly trap.

The barn showed no sign of either of the Dahlquists. He kept looking. The only sign of real habitation came from the bathhouse. Someone had heated water and left the soapy bathwater in the tub. If Slocum had to guess, he would say Marcus was the one who had bathed and not tidied up after himself.

Outside the bathhouse, he looked around before heading to the fields. At the corner of the wheat field he heard the familiar sound of a hoe hacking away at weeds. Walking faster, he went along the edge of the field until he saw Laura bent over the hoe, working furiously as if the weeds would spring up if she slowed. Slocum had to smile. It always seemed that way. Crops required nurturing, as weeds were tenacious in the way they crowded out everything else unless chopped.

She looked up as he made his way down the row. She brushed back the dark hair dangling into her eyes, then grinned. Dropping the hoe, she ran to him with arms outstretched. Laura almost bowled him over as she threw her arms around his neck and swung herself about.

He caught her at the waist and set her down.

"I thought I'd never see you again, John. You came back."

"I got tied up with some unexpected business," he said. "Have you seen anything of Monty Turner or any of his gang?"

"No, nothing. Is that why you returned? Turner is coming back to Bitter Creek?"

"He might be hightailing out of Indian Territory," Slocum said. "Detectives from the railroad will make this country too hot for him."

"It's almost too hot for me, and I mean the temperature," she said, swiping at more sweat. "Let's go back to the house. I can use something to drink."

"Where's your brother?"

"He left early this morning," Laura said. "He didn't say, but I think he went to town. He was . . . happy."

"Unnaturally so?" Slocum suspected this was the case. Marcus's moods swung faster than the pendulum on a big Regulator wall clock.

"I hesitate to say that," she said cautiously. "It's better than when he is in a dark mood. He gets violent then. But since Cora has been . . . gone, he's more cheerful."

A question danced on the tip of Slocum's tongue. He didn't want to ask but did anyway.

"Cora and Marcus never saw eye to eye, did they?"

"Why do you say that?"

"She was going to marry Hop Franks. He got killed. When she took up with Joe Bench, she got shot. Did Cora even want to come work on the farm?"

"She didn't, but there was nowhere for her to stay if she remained in St. Louis. Marcus convinced her to come to Bitter Creek. What are you getting at, John?"

"Nothing much," he said, thinking of all the folks who had died, mostly with bullets in the back.

"Come on in and cool off. Let me get that pitcher of water I set out this morning."

He watched her leave the front room and go to the kitchen. Her clothing was plastered to her body with sweat and every move showed a new contour. Slocum couldn't help reflecting what a beautiful woman she was.

"Here, John, here's some— Oh! I'm sorry!"

Slocum jumped back but the water from the pitcher spilled all over him, gluing his clothes to him the same way

Laura's were. She put down the pitcher and pressed her hands into his chest, squeezing out the water. It ran down his chest, tickling as it went. She looked up and he wondered if she had spilled the water on him intentionally.

It hardly mattered. He kissed her. Their bodies melted together, wet and warm and demanding. Before he knew it, he was stripping her matted clothes off her body. And she was doing the same task for him. The warm breeze blew through the house but did nothing to cool their bodies or their passions.

Amid the kissing and undressing, they sank to the floor, arms still wrapped around one another. Slocum was the first to break off the kiss to put his mouth to better use. He licked along her sweat-salty jaw line and lower, to her arching neck, and even farther down to the deep valley between her firm breasts. She tasted fine to him, of work and sex and the utter essence of woman. He caught one taut red button in his lips and suckled. Laura moaned in delight at this. He gently gnawed and released it, letting it spring back. He moved to the other cherry nub of flesh capping this breast and repeated the action. He felt tremors pass through her body as she seemed to melt to the floor. He followed her down, his mouth continuing to give her as much stimulation as he could.

By the time Laura lay on her back, Slocum was achingly hard and ready. He moved his hand between her clenched thighs and gently parted them. His fingers slipped along her nether lips and felt the dampness flowing from within. She was ready for him. He moved into the vee formed by her long, slender white legs and pressed forward. For a moment the plum-tip of his manhood slid all about and then he found the proper spot. He arched his back and slid easily into her hungering depths.

Slocum was carried away by the sheer feel of the female flesh around him. Laura tensed and gave him an insistent massage using only her inner muscles. He pulled back, looked down into her half-closed eyes, and knew he could never hold back.

"Go on, John. Take me. I want you so much!" She reached out and gripped his upper arms fiercely. Her fingernails cut into his flesh, spurring him on. His hips moved with a will of their own. He sank back into her heated core but this time he did not linger. He withdrew immediately, only to push forward again. His hips moved faster until he was on fire. From the way she thrashed about under him, she felt the blaze, too.

Faster, harder, he thrust into her. She lifted her ass off the floor to take him even deeper with every thrust. She locked her heels behind his back, making sure he could not escape—as if he wanted to!

Grunting, striving, they moved together in the age-old rhythm until Slocum was unable to continue. Warmth turned to fire in his loins. The fire became superheated and erupted like molten lava while she gasped and pressed herself down hard around him. Greedy for sensation, they rode one another until there was nothing left but satiation.

Slocum collapsed beside Laura on the floor. She rolled over, her naked breasts pressed to his bare chest. Their faces were inches apart as she said, "I wish this could last forever. But it won't."

Slocum said nothing. She realized that they belonged in different worlds. Even if she stayed on the farm, Slocum had no interest in bringing in a crop year after year. When he had been at home on Slocum's Stand, the farming had been the hardest work of all. Although he had been an excellent farmer, he preferred hunting—being free to move on when the wind blew him away. Being prisoner to a plot of land—and even a woman as lovely as Laura Dahlquist—wasn't the way Slocum wanted to live. It wasn't the way he *could* live.

"I don't know when Marcus will be back," Laura said, heaving a deep sigh. "I don't even know where he went, but I don't think it would be a good idea for him to find us like this."

Slocum played with one nipple and then kissed it. He sat up.

"You're right."

"You're not even going to argue with me about it?" Laura sounded disappointed, but Slocum saw the acceptance of the way things had to be in her face.

They dressed slowly, Slocum wringing out the water in his clothes into a vase on the table by the door. Laura was more discreet and wrung out her clothes in the kitchen before dressing and returning.

"John, I can't find my barrette," she said, patting her mussed hair and looking distraught. "It is silver and was my mama's. I think I left it out at the bathhouse this morning. Could you look for me? I'll fix some more cool water."

"I hope your aim's better this time," Slocum said, smiling.

"It can't match yours," Laura replied.

Slocum took his time going to the bathhouse to look around. This gave him time to think about what he might be passing up by riding out and leaving Laura behind to tend the farm with her brother. Inside the bathhouse he saw the table where Laura placed her belongings as she bathed. The hair clip had fallen to the ground to one side of the table and was partially hidden by a muddy footprint. From the size, it had to be Marcus's. Slocum bent and picked up the hair clip, then froze.

The sound of horses galloping into the yard alerted Slocum to gathering trouble. He placed the barrette on the table and slipped out of the bathhouse to cautiously peer around the side. A half dozen men dressed in frock coats and wearing bowlers dismounted. Marcus Dahlquist came up after them, his horse not able to keep the pace of the others.

"You sure the son of a bitch is here?" demanded the bulkiest of the well-dressed riders. He had a potbelly barely constrained by his vest. A huge walrus mustache quivered as he spoke. Bushy muttonchops and a jutting, truculent chin finished the picture for Slocum. This was a man used to high living—and being in charge, no matter where he was.

"He rides with Turner, and Turner's in the vicinity," Marcus said.

"Mr. Gibbons is not paying us for wild-goose chases. He demands action. Are you sure this Slocum fellow is a member of the gang and can lead us to Turner?"

"He's Turner's right-hand man. I'm sure he's killed more'n his share of railroad conductors and engineers, too."

"What he has done is less important to Mr. Gibbons than stopping future depredation," the mustached detective said. He twirled the tips and looked around. "He's here? This Slocum fellow?"

"He's hiding," Marcus said. "He's a coward and likely to shoot you in the back, but he's here and can tell you where to find Turner."

"That's the important detail," the detective said. He motioned for his men to circle the house.

Slocum knew it would take the detectives a few minutes to figure he wasn't in the house. Whether Laura would tell them he was out hunting for a piece of her jewelry was something he couldn't decide—and he wasn't going to stick around to find out. Eventually the detectives would search the rest of the property, no matter what Laura said or didn't. Marcus would egg them on.

Fuming at Marcus's treachery, Slocum led his horse out the side door and swung into the saddle. Walking the horse slowly toward the fields with the head-high wheat, he kept the barn between him and the farmhouse. When he got into the field he picked up the pace, and when he reached the far side of the field, he galloped away. The hilly country in the direction of Hop Franks's offered the best chance for hiding. If the detectives began a search, Slocum would give them a difficult hunt.

He doubted they had the stomach for that since Monty Turner was the real target for their manhunt.

The way Marcus Dahlquist had fetched the railroad detectives and brought them to the farm specifically to arrest Slocum rankled, though. A lot.

19

Slocum didn't ride far. He found himself a hollow and dismounted, letting his mare drink from a shallow pond while he sat on a stump and fumed at what Marcus Dahlquist had done. There was no call for him to go to the detectives the way he had. Monty Turner was the source of all the trouble, not John Slocum.

"Maybe that's not the problem," Slocum said aloud. The mare looked up, a large brown eye fixed on him. "Might be I've been looking at everything all wrong." He fell silent and the horse went back to drinking as Slocum thought hard on everything that had happened to him since he had ridden into Indian Territory.

When the horse had drunk enough, Slocum pulled her away and mounted. He could hide, wait for the detectives to leave, and then talk to Laura again, but their fat leader wasn't likely to pass up any chance to find Turner. He would leave behind one of his men to spy on Laura and the farm, waiting for Slocum to show up again.

There was another way to work through what was going on and find out if he was right about the troubles at the

179

Dahlquist farm. Slocum circled a hill and made his way to the summit where he looked down over the farm. Using his field glasses, he made out the detectives standing in a tight knot, arguing with Marcus. He didn't have to be close enough to eavesdrop to know what was being said. The portly detective was laying down the law to Marcus about leading them on a wild-goose chase.

And, as Slocum had guessed, when the detectives rode away, they stopped a hundred yards down the road and one of them was sent to a gully to stand watch if Slocum ever returned. He swung his field glasses back and saw Laura and Marcus arguing. She stamped her foot, then spun about and went back into the house. Marcus threw his hands up in the air and then mounted his horse and rode off.

From the direction he took, Slocum figured Marcus Dahlquist was returning to Bitter Creek. Slocum judged distances and how fast Marcus was riding and knew the young man would reach town before he could get off the hill and circle about so he wouldn't be seen by the detective left to capture him. While he might sneak up on the detective and get rid of him, either permanently or temporarily by tying him up, Slocum decided it was better to scatter his enemies across the countryside rather than remove them from the game.

Riding doggedly, Slocum reached Bitter Creek a couple hours later. The only thing he could say about his ride was that nobody had spotted him. He entered town cautiously, wondering if the detectives had come to Bitter Creek or had gone back to the railroad tracks to hunt for Turner. If the outlaw had heard of the detectives coming after him, he ought to have hightailed it out of Indian Territory by now. Slocum wondered where Turner had hidden the gold from the train robbery. It seemed to be a waste to steal that much gold only for revenge against the railroad owner.

Slocum left his horse behind the bank and walked

around, peering inside through the gaps in the boarded windows. Nobody had bothered to replace the broken glass and, if they had not done so by now, nobody ever would. The teller was alone. Slocum looked up and down the street and saw a few people stirring. Monty Turner's threats still gripped the town. Slocum slipped into the dimly lit bank lobby. The teller looked up, eyes going wide. He reached for a pistol but did not pull it from under the counter.

"Didn't expect to see you again," the teller said. He looked around nervously. Slocum rested his hand on the butt of his six-shooter to emphasize how wrong it would be for the teller to show his weapon.

"Have the railroad detectives been here asking after . . . Turner?" Slocum watched the teller's reaction closely.

"Detectives? Hell, no, but Marcus Dahlquist was here. See? See the holes in the ceiling? He came in, started talking crazy, and then began shooting. I thought he was going to kill me."

Slocum didn't look up. To have done so might have emboldened the teller to whip out his six-gun.

"How long ago?"

"Half hour." The teller took a deep breath, looked over at the still-unopened safe, and said, "I can't get the safe company to send me the combination. I could blow it open. Mostly, I think I'll leave town and find a job somewhere else."

"With gents going loco like Dahlquist, that might be a good idea," Slocum said. He wanted to ask again if the detectives had been here, but he held back. There wasn't any reason to alert the teller that a reward might be in the offing if he got some backbone and used his pistol.

"You couldn't open that vault, could you, Mr. Slocum?" The teller licked his lips nervously. "We . . . we could split whatever's in it. We'd deserve it. Goodman owed me more than he ever paid, and for you, it's got to be a useful skill worth getting paid to blow a safe."

"All right," Slocum said. "I need to get some equipment. You got an account at the general store?"

His answer took the teller by surprise. Then a broad, silly grin crossed his face.

"I do. You charge it all, whatever you need. It's in Mr. Goodman's name but the store owner's all right with me running up the bill. Especially after he was killed like that. Mr. Goodman, I mean." The teller was sweating profusely. It was a hot day, but his nerves added rivers to the perspiration already pouring down his face.

Slocum wondered if the sudden case of nerves came from deciding to rob the bank and saying to hell with Bitter Creek and its citizens or if he played for time. If the detectives had been here, the teller might be thinking he could earn a little reward by turning Slocum over to them.

"I'll be back in an hour or so," Slocum said, lying. He had no intention of blowing open the safe. If he ever did want to try it, why split with the teller? He stepped out into the street and heard gunfire from the direction of the pharmacy. Slocum stepped back onto the boardwalk and pressed close to the bank wall as he saw Marcus come from the pharmacy, waving around his six-shooter and doing a strange dance in the middle of the street.

"I'm ten feet tall and there's nowhere in town that can fit me with boots!" Marcus laughed and shot out a window. The tinkling of broken glass hid whatever he said next. Slocum didn't much care since it was all crazy talk. If Marcus had had a breakfast of loco weed, he couldn't have been acting any stranger.

The young man reloaded his six-shooter and went down the middle of the street, taking potshots at anyone who dared poke their nose out.

"I'm ready to lasso a tornado and herd goats!" His strange cries were punctuated with more lead sailing through the walls of the Bitter Creek buildings.

Slocum could have removed him as a danger to the

townspeople, but he figured they could deal with Marcus on their own. Their lives and property were at stake. Why should he pull their fat from the fire? He had a more burning question to answer, one that repeated in his mind as he fetched his horse and rode from Bitter Creek listening to the dying echoes from Marcus's pistol.

He considered taking out the detective who had been left as lookout but knew this would alert the rest of the railroad dicks to his presence. He wanted them occupied with Monty Turner and his gang, not dogging John Slocum's tracks. Slocum approached the farm through the fields, using the wheat as cover. The slight wind blowing covered his movement as he walked his horse toward the barn. It provided a screen unless the detective had moved, and Slocum doubted he had. The man didn't look as if he had a great deal of initiative. Told to stay, he would sit like a good hunting dog and wait to point.

Slocum entered the farmhouse through the kitchen door, paused, and listened hard. If Laura was in the house, he didn't hear her. Walking on cat's feet, he went to the front room and the rolltop desk. He knew which drawer to open. It slid wide and he simply stared.

The six-shooter that had belonged to Marcus's pa still rested in the drawer. Slocum picked it up and ran his finger over its barrel. The pistol had not been fired—but Marcus had one in town and was firing wildly using it. He opened the gate and saw that it was still unloaded. He carefully fit six bullets into the chambers, closed the gate, and stared at the pistol. Slocum returned the six-gun to the drawer and closed it softly.

He checked the front of the house, peering through the lace curtains, but didn't see the detective. Walking quickly, Slocum went back to the barn and rummaged through the tools until he found a shovel. He sat and stared at it for a spell, wondering if what he intended on doing was the right thing to do. When he reached the point of having to know, he stood and picked up the shovel. This might be wrong, but he had to settle things once and for all.

Slocum made his way back to the field, then angled through to reach the hill overlooking the farm where the Dahlquist family had started the small cemetery. The dirt was still mounded over Cora's grave. Rain and wind and the weight of time would eventually compact that dirt and let the grass grow over her grave.

But it wasn't Cora's grave that drew him. The grass had already spread over both of the other graves. Slocum began digging, throwing dirt aside into a pile until he had dug down five feet to what proved to be Laura and Marcus's mother. There was no stench from the corpse since it had been buried long enough to let the worms chew away anything that might decay. He gripped the edges of the blanket she was buried in, then hesitated.

He hesitated, remembering stories of blankets infected with smallpox and other diseases. If she had died of influenza, Slocum might catch it. Germs could survive long after the body they killed.

Slocum took a deep breath, then heaved the body up and out of the grave. He rolled it over and gingerly unwrapped the blanket. He didn't have to be a doctor to figure out the woman's cause of death. A small hole in the back of her skull had turned into a big one on her forehead. She had been shot in the back of the head. She might have had the flu, but there was no way anyone could have survived such a gunshot.

Taking care, Slocum reburied her and then began digging up her husband. It took Slocum longer because he knew what he would find. And he did.

The man's body tumbled out of the blanket in two pieces. A slug had shattered his spine. Slocum poked through the remains and saw that this man had died from a gunshot to the back, also. From the evidence, it seemed that more than one round had ripped through the back.

Slocum dropped his shovel and wiped his hands off on his jeans, then froze when he heard a six-shooter cocking.

"Don't go for it, Slocum. You do that and I swear, you'll be worm food. I'll do it, I will!"

"Why not?" Slocum said. "You murdered your parents. You shot them in the back. Why?"

"They wanted to give up on the farm. I couldn't let them do that. They were crazy to do it. That would have stolen my inheritance!"

"As the only son, you'd have inherited. But you don't know anything about farming, Marcus. Why do you want to hang on to the farm?"

"Nobody ever gave me credit for doing anything because I'm the youngest. I'll show them. They turned on me. So I shot them!"

"Like you did Cora? Why'd you kill her?" Slocum hesitated, then knew the answer. "Because she was sweet on Bench. You killed Hop Franks to keep him from taking over your farm, no matter how bad you'd run it."

"She was a traitor! She did it to cross me. The only way to stop her was to kill her. I had to do it to teach her a lesson."

"But you shot her in the back. Couldn't you at least have faced her? Cora was your sister, dammit!"

"You're like the rest. You . . . you don't understand."

"Ernest Goodman? You killed the banker, too," Slocum pressed on. "Why'd you do that? He was going to arrange for a buyer for the farm."

"He didn't talk to *me*. He told you about a buyer. *You*. He expected you to marry Laura and be the one running the farm. I didn't matter to him, so I killed him."

"You robbed him to make it look like somebody else did it. I should have known right away. Who would gun down a man—or a woman—by backshooting them? Turner might be a snake in the grass, but he's not a coward. Not like that."

"You shut up. You can't understand."

"So you'll have to shoot me. In the back. That's murder, Marcus. Let me—"

Slocum was already moving, but his foot slipped on the edge of the grave he had opened. He tumbled forward, arms flailing. A shot sounded, echoed, died. Slocum spun around, fighting to get his six-shooter out. He sat up in the open grave to a scene he had not expected.

Laura Dahlquist stood holding a smoking six-shooter in both hands. She stared at her brother, sprawled facedown on the ground.

"I shot him," she said in a choked voice.

"He would have killed me, like he did your parents. Like he did Cora."

"I shot my own brother in the back." She turned desolate eyes toward him. Slocum scrambled out of the grave and slid his Colt Navy back into its holster. He gently took the pistol from her nerveless fingers. It was her pa's six-shooter that he had returned to the desk drawer.

"You saved my life. Thank you."

Laura grabbed his arms and buried her face in his chest. Hot tears soaked into his shirt while Slocum held her awkwardly. It took a few minutes before Laura stopped quaking and stepped away from him. Her blue eyes were bloodshot and tears had left dusty tracks down her cheeks.

"What am I going to do, John? What can I do?"

Slocum knelt and rummaged through Marcus's pockets. The few dollars there and a gold watch might well have been all that was left from killing and robbing the banker. Slocum flipped open the watch case and saw Goodman's name engraved there. He closed it and tucked it back into Marcus's pocket.

"Here," he said, handing the money to Laura. He remembered the deed he had taken from Goodman's files showing the farm was all paid off. He took this rumpled, dirty paper from his pocket and gave it to her. "The money'll tide you over. You can find someone in town to buy the farm. The deed shows it's your property to sell. You won't get much but you can return to St. Louis."

"Why?" She wandered around aimlessly, going from one grave to the next and finally returning to Marcus's body. "Why shouldn't I stay here?"

"You don't belong," Slocum said gently. He didn't like the notion of Laura staying in the house where she could see the hill where her parents and sister were buried—and where she had shot her brother in the back.

"I should go," she said dully.

"I'll bury him. There's no reason for anyone in town to know what happened."

"Yes, bury him. He doesn't deserve it, but he should be buried."

Slocum returned Laura's father to his grave, then dug a new one for Marcus. It took the better part of an hour, but he was in no hurry and the day was hot. He kept one eye peeled for the detective to come up the hill to find the source of the gunshot, but the detective had either left his post or had figured it wasn't worth stirring from the shade on such a humid day.

He tamped down the last of the dirt on top of Marcus Dahlquist. He refrained from spitting on the grave because Laura still watched.

"Thank you," she said. She turned and walked down the hill with leaden steps.

Slocum saw no reason to go after her. He got his mare and rode due west, hoping he could put enough distance between him and the troubles on the farm to forget. He couldn't.